THE MIND

AND THE SECRET OF RECEIVING MONEY

amar

Invincible Publishers

First published in India in 2018

ISBN: 978-93-87328-85-3

Invincible Publishers

G-120, Sushant Lok III, Sector 57, Gurgaon-122002

Registered Address: Opposite Kasturba Ashram,
Radaur, Haryana - 135133

Cover Design: Ashish Samant

My deepest gratitude to my dh and to my all 7.4 + billions .

Acknowledgement

The Bhagavad Gita has been my Inspiration since a very young age. I started reading the book, 'The Bhagavad Gita According to Gandhi' written by Mahadev Desai in 1988 .

The Book as well as Gandhi ji's principles have had a deep impression on my mind.

I read the book regularly and tried to follow its values in my daily life.

I tried to know and understand detachment or non-attachment from Bhagavad Gita and gave it the term FREE. I experimented with the teachings and ideas of the Bhagavad Gita and found them TRUE.

The best ideas I got from the Bhagavad Gita are -

Action alone is thy province, never the fruits.

Along with the book and Gandhi ji, Love was my inspiration.

Love will always be my inspiration.

Loving all the 7.4+ billions of the world, loving your belief, loving the person you love.

Loving your belief is the highest form of LOVE.

Preface

No fundamental statements described in this book should be interpreted as being intended to interfere directly or indirectly with any man or woman's religious habits.

This book has been confined exclusively to guide the reader to understand the harmonious schedules to ACCEPT an IDEA which gives us our DESIRE.

Bhagavad Gita Quotes are from "The Bhagavad Gita According to Gandhi"

by Mohandas K. Gandhi (Author), Mahadev Desai (Trasnslator)

(Bhagavad Gita: Chapter Two, verse 47: "Karmany vadhikaras te, ma phalesu kadachana ma karma-phala-hetur bhur, ma te sango 'stv akarmani."

Action alone is thy province, never the fruits thereof.

–Bhagavad Gita

Free plays the RESULTS (fruits) part for YOU.

RECEIVE ALL in REALITY as soon as YOU ACCEPT the following IDEA:

"MONEY, health, happiness, harmonious relationships and a harmonious life come to us by THEMSELVES when YOU / SELF-become(s) FREE from all.

YOU / SELF-become(s) FREE from all just by ACCEPTANCE."

"Karmany-evadhikaras-te,Ma-phalesu-kadachana ma karma-phala-hetur bhur, ma te sango 'stv akarmani."

(Bhagwad Gita: Chapter Two, verse 47)

Action alone is thy province, never the fruits thereof.– Bhagavad Gita

It never means to leave RESULTS, but the absence of attachment with them. As a matter of fact, by doing so, we reap a thousand fold RESULTS.

"yada yada hi dharmasya, glanir bhavati Bharata

abhyutthanam adharmasya tadatmanam srjamy aham"

(Bhagavad Gita: Chapter Four, verse 7)

Whenever righteousness declines and the purpose of life is forgotten, I manifest myself to protect and re-establish righteousness.

Contents

1

The SUPREME Schedule (0–14 years of age)

We were born FREE from all. We were one (connected) with the billions and the Supreme. And we were full of Gratitude.

Every religion believes that we lived in paradise once, and then it got lost, so we start searching for it again.

As soon as our senses come in contact with objects, we develop desires and thoughts. Then, we lose contact or disconnect with that paradise of being free from all, of being one with the billions and the SUPREME, and enjoying the fullness of Gratitude.

So, from the SS (0- 14 years of age) we enter the PS (14–30 years of age).

There are five schedules in our life –

1. The Supreme Schedule: The SS (0- 14 years of age)– Free, one with the Supreme, full of Gratitude- FREE level 3 / HC level 3

2. The Preparing Schedule : The PS (14–30 years of age)–Mainly about Aim / Preparing our HC–Free level 1 / HC level 1

3. The Receiving Schedule: The RS (30–40 years of age)–Mainly about the Knowledge of the FREE-HC and getting READY for RESULTS–Free level 2 / HC level 2

4. The Supreme Schedule: The SS (40 +–till last 80 +)–Mainly consists of RECEIVING our HC / RESULTS & Free level 4 -HC–Free level 3 / HC level 3

5. The POS Schedule (after-life i.e., after 80+)–All HC completed

HC means a harmonious combination of Aim/Money/ Purpose

As soon as we (our senses) come in contact with objects, we grow desires; desires bring thoughts; and thus, the thoughts/desires overtake the FREE.

It disconnects us from the billions, the Supreme, and the fullness of gratitude goes down. We have come down from the paradise to a lower state -

1. With the fullness of Gratitude, we have come down to FAITH (faith is born of Gratitude).

2. From oneness with the billions and the Supreme, we have come to Mind and EGO.

3. From being FREE from all, we have come down to having THOUGHTS and Desires of wealth (MONEY **+), health, happiness, harmonious relationships and a harmonious life.**

Now we are attached to desire. The only way to be FREE from all again is through desires only. We can't

leave the desire; if we leave one desire, another will come up and so on.

So, the only way to be FREE from all again is through desire.

HC (HARMONIOUS COMBINATION)

As we beget desires, we move from the SS (0- 14 years of age) to enter the PS (14–30 years of age).

Since we have desires, we should make a right combination of our desires in the PS.

Money is one of the most strongest desires.

We should combine our Aim, along with the Purpose, with MONEY.

Only MONEY, leaving the AIM and the Purpose; or sole Aim, leaving the Money and the Purpose; or only the Purpose, leaving the Aim and Money, is not complete.

So, we should make a combination of these three.

A harmonious combination (HC) of these three: Aim, Money Purpose, helps to GET, KEEP and STAY growing in these three areas.

Mainly, the Preparing Schedule (PS: 14–30 years of age) is for preparing the Aim, but it could as well be utilised for developing a Mindset for Money and preparing the highest emotion with our purpose, i.e., faith in aim, money, and the purpose.

Combining MONEY with our AIM and the Purpose) and then writing it is called a Harmonious Combination.

So, we know by our HC what we are going to do and have in life.

AIM – MONEY – PURPOSE

Most of us focus on things we don't really want because we do not decide our HC. So, by writing down our HC, we move away from the things which we don't want towards the things we want.

For example, we think we don't want to be poor.

Instead, we should think, I want to be RICH and make an HC.

On the other side, most of us don't know what we want. So, by combining MONEY with our AIM and Purpose, and then writing it, makes us know what we really want. When we get FREE from all again, we should know what we want. Know -

What do we want to be/do.

How much money do we want to have.

What is our purpose.

Know it and write it down.

Set the biggest desires (Aim), the most Money and the biggest Purpose .

Make a combination of Aim and Purpose with Money.

We don't need to think of how to get our HC or the RESULTS (FRUITS), FREE plays the RESULTS part of the HC for us.

Most of us don't write because we think we can't get it.

Yes, we can't because that's not our part; FREE gets it for us.

Action alone is thy province, never the fruits thereof.

–Bhagavad Gita

Our part is to write it and to prepare it only. It seems easy now, so set the biggest HC and write it.

1. Money–How much money do you want for your product/net worth? (the most)

2. AIM–what do you want to be do?......................... (the biggest)

3. Purpose–................................. (the biggest)

Along with the desire for the most Money and the biggest Aim in life, we should have the biggest Purpose in life too; the biggest purpose, the biggest aim and the most money.

Now, it becomes the biggest HC. FREE is capable of getting the biggest HC.

Have the biggest HC because when we are FREE again, we should know what our HC is and FREE will get it for you.

Moreover, a small or big HC takes more or less the same effort, so why not have the biggest HC, and when FREE plays the RESULT part for us, **just prepare your HC in the PS** (14–30 years of age). ***Action alone is thy province, not the results.***

The moment we read these wonderful lines form the GITA, the thought comes to our mind, 'Why only ACTION (hard work, practice), when we can't think of the RESULTS?'

Of course we can think of the results, but FREE will get the results for us. Our part is to prepare our HC in the PS.

Thinking about the RESULTS (of how we will get it) is not our part.

FREE plays the RESULTS part for us.

The Mind does the preparing part of our HC for us;

FREE plays the RESULTS part for us.

Just write it down, write the biggest HC.

Writing your HC is 90% of the work done.

Our HC has Money, Aim and Purpose, as well as the HC related things, i.e., health, happiness, harmonious relationships and a harmonious life in it.

So great is our HC.

AIM-

Find out what you like to do/be the most. It could be anything good in which you have an active interest–business, music, sports, art, etc. Even a hobby counts.

Explore your qualities and skills, or what you think is essential for you.

Ask yourself what you love to do/be. Knowing what we're good at maximizes our talent. The Aim is the seed of the Ultimate Aim. We all may have different Aims, but the Purpose is the same for all–**to serve others.**

Set the Aim in line with the Purpose. Set a noble Aim.

Know your good qualities and strengths which will help you as well as the others.

Knowing our strengths enables us to focus on what we can excel at. Choose what you want to do with your new awareness. Our Aim, with MONEY and Purpose linked to it, becomes the biggest.

Set an Aim, a significant objective in your HC.

Write down your AIM -

1.Best one

2....

3....

4....

5.Hobby

MONEY -

Money is the strongest desire in today's world.

It is good. We should desire money.

We should have money.

We cannot survive well without money.

We all have the desire for big money.

We should combine our desire for MONEY with our Aim and the Purpose to make a harmonious combination(HC).

We should start preparing for our HC.

An HC preparing schedule is given in the oncoming chapter.

Scientists say that everything is either matter or energy.

Money is energy.

Ideas are energy. Energy attracts energy.

Our HC is full of energy. Everything we create or acquire begins in the form of desire. Our most active desire in today's world is money.

Money itself is a great inspiration.

The desire for money becomes harmonious when we combine this desire with our Aim and the Purpose. In this way, we make a significant HC.

Have a spiritual relation with MONEY.

Do not have any misconceptions about desiring money.

We are not taught well about wanting money and it is not taught in our schools either.

Most of us do not set a high HC and do not desire big money due to the misconceptions and bondages (questions/worry/fear/doubt) regarding HC and money.

Those who have earned big money understand money well.

Money comes to those who have a desire for money with a good Purpose .

That is why we set an HC. Set big money in your HC. Our HC is great; we gain Everything along with HC. We also gain health, happiness, harmonious relationships and a harmonious life with it.

The number of self-made millionaires and billionaires is on the rise every year. Maybe, we feel guilty about thinking about money because we have heard or have been taught that money is the root of all evil. But there are many ways for Money to be spiritual .i.e., if we have a lot of money, we may help those who don't have it by creating resources for them.

Money is good. It is up to us how we use it. If we use it in a reasonable manner for ourselves and for helping others, it can be the best tool. Money helps us and many others to have a better life. We should develop a sense of spirituality with money, and have an abundance of material things through our HC.

Enjoy being RICH. Start having a good relation with Money by developing good habits like having a piggy-bank. Start at a small level, e.g., with just one dollar. Imagine getting a dollar richer with it. Enjoy the feeling of being just a little bit richer than you were before.

Fill your mind with the thoughts of people who achieved abundance in their lives. There is more than enough money for every single person. Read about the successful and rich people who have shared their success stories in books, newspaper, etc. We deserve to be RICH.

Money is the value of our actions, our knowledge.

Get rid of all the misconceptions about Money. We may have some limiting beliefs about money;

know them and ask yourself,

'Why do I believe in these limiting beliefs about Money?

What if I did not believe in them?'

And thus, change your limiting beliefs to those of abundance of Money with your HC.

There is an increase in the number of millionaires in the world every year. Many of the richest people in the world didn't have the highest grades. I mean to say that education is a way to increase one's knowledge, but low or average grades never stop us from being RICH. Even if we did not have good grades, education never prevents us from being RICH; the important thing is how we use the knowledge which we have gained through studying or learning from the surroundings.

Most successful people are 40+, so age is not a bar. The 40+ age is especially the best age to be RICH, but we need to prepare for it from the start. We don't always need money to make money. Many have started from scratch, lived in small rooms and did part-time jobs. We don't need to master the knowledge of a business to start; we may just start at a tiny scale and then grow gradually. At the same time, we gain knowledge gradually too. Just change your thinking.

You might not be rich enough right now, but just change your thinking from 'survival and security' to 'wealth and abundance' and wealth and abundance with become your HC.

Getting rich is hard work, but we are already doing hard work. Then why not set Money in our HC, so that our hard work moves us towards making us RICH.

In the PS (Preparing Schedule), we prepare for our HC. PS is a little hard work, but the next two schedules–the RS (Receiving Schedule) and the SS (Supreme Schedule) are very easy.

We don't really need to do anything in the RS and the SS, and our HC comes to us by ITSELF. Most of us think that it is hard all throughout the life; that's why most people don't set the biggest HC. However, know that we don't need to do anything in the RS and the SS, and our HC comes to us by ITSELF.

Be AWARE of all that you have heard about money, wealth and rich people. And make a new spiritual relationship with Money. When we use our money, it goes through hundreds of people. So, we are ultimately helping each other grow RICH.

We should make ourselves a role model for others, as a kind and charitable rich person. Money just requires a little hard work in the PS, and we might even enjoy a lot along with the hard work in the PS. We don't need to choose between two things for the sake of money.

Our HC will lead us to be RICH. Money helps us have the freedom of time. Money lets us enjoy the things we like in life, and makes us capable of helping others as well.

A millionaire is someone who knows he/she will become a millionaire, but they want to do it on their own terms, with an Aim they like the most, and a great purpose for it.

There are many ways to become a millionaire, but creating our own business (product) is one of the best ways to be rich and wealthy. We may start from scratch (with very less investment) or from a start-up level.

Health, happiness, harmonious relationships, a harmonious life and wealth (Money + net worth) is called RICHES, and all of them are here in ABUNDANCE.

We can have them in abundance.

"You can serve God and man in no more effective way than by getting rich."

-Wallace D. Wattles.

"If you want to help the poor, demonstrate to them that they can become rich, prove it to them by getting rich yourself."

PURPOSE

Our Aim and Money should have an Purpose, a social motive.

It is the social responsibility to help the people who do not have money.

We connect with a billion others through our ultimate aim. We all know that a big segment of the population is not rich.

Over-population might be one of the reasons. We can contribute to this by controlling the population. The population should grow in the right proportion.

Youngsters should think better about it. Doing so, everyone will have employment and all shall have the natural and material resources to enjoy life. The coming generation will then be rich enough and everyone will have some social motive which is beneficial to the society as their ultimate aim. When a person does not have money and is unemployed, he does not think of the HC.

He thinks only of food, clothing, and shelter. The government alone cannot make us all rich. We all should take on this social responsibility; our ultimate aim should be to give riches to all.

Be RICH and contribute a part of your wealth to them in some form, so that they can become capable too and go on to set their HC, and make others capable in their turn.

Our HC has Money, AIM, and PURPOSE; it covers health, happiness, harmonious relationships and a harmonious life as well. Our minds are capable of preparing our HC. We should prepare our minds for our HC.

We should make a harmonious combination of our desire for money with our aim and the Purpose. Then, our mind shall begin to prepare for their harmonious combination. Most of us do not have big money. But, if we have a desire for money in our HC, our wonderful MIND will give us all billions.

We should prepare our minds within.

We should ready our minds for the infinite and the limitless.

We should create limitlessness in our minds.

MIND

Our Mind is divided into two parts-

1. Finite mind or conscious mind

2. Subconscious mind

1. Finite Mind or Conscious Mind -

The finite mind is the thinking part of our mind. This section begets all THOUGHTS.

When we are young, our FINITE MIND is very active. MILLIONS of thoughts come and go through our finite mind. As our Mind comes in contact with objects or desires, we get related thoughts in the finite mind to form objectives or aspirations. We should then make a harmonious combination for our DESIRES with the AIM, Money, and PURPOSE, and set our harmonious combination (HC) accordingly.

By placing an HC in life, we get thoughts related to our HC in our mind.

Let's call them HC thoughts.

Thereby, the non-HC thoughts become secondary because if we keep our mind open, many non–HC thoughts come and go through our Finite Mind.

HC thoughts are related to our HC, i.e., to our aim, money, and purpose + our health, happiness, harmonious relationships and a harmonious life. When we have everything good in our HC and HC related thoughts, we don't need the non-HC thoughts. We should let the HC related thoughts come into our mind.

We should hold the HC related thoughts in our mind by chanting them over and over again. Thus, we do not allow the non–HC thoughts to come to our mind. Chanting the HC related thoughts in our mind is the extra effort which we should do for our biggest HC. This is the preparation within our minds for our HC.

The Finite Mind is very active at a young age.

It is the right time to give the thoughts of HC to our FINITE mind by following and chanting of thoughts related to our HC in our Mind. It makes our mind understand what we want to prepare for.

We should also constantly act on these HC related thoughts.

The finite mind/conscious mind is active when we are young. We think approximately 60,000 thoughts per day. 95% or more of these thoughts are had unconsciously, i.e., we are not aware of what we are thinking.

But, if we set our HC then we are consciously think the HC thoughts and feelings only, and thus the non-HC thoughts and feelings won't enter our mind. Our HC related thoughts are all the good thoughts, things, and beliefs related to our HC. HC thoughts are related to our HC as well as all other good thoughts that are indirectly related to our HC. Rest all other thoughts are secondary thoughts or non-HC thoughts which don't belong to our HC.

The sub-conscious mind analyzes the thoughts and feelings which we enjoy, repeat and hold, and then forms behavioral habits and beliefs based on those thoughts and feelings. For example, if we are following/chanting HC thoughts consciously, it means we are consciously growing FAITH in our HC and in our SC Mind (Subconscious Mind).

If we are not following/chanting HC thoughts, our mind may follow the non-HC thoughts unconsciously. Non-HC thoughts grow a Bondage (unnecessary worry, fear, doubt, questions) against our HC. Thus, the conscious mind continually focusses on the fear, worry, and doubt about our HC, attaching a feeling/emotion to it (worry, doubt, fear, questions) and stores it in the subconscious mind. This worry, fear, doubt, question, which is just a perception, is saved as a behavior, a habit and a belief in the subconscious during the PS (The Preparing Schedule), which becomes a non-HC behavior pattern, habit, and belief in the RS (The Receiving Schedule).

So, set the HC (Aim, Money, Purpose) and write it, so it becomes solid, then follow only the HC thoughts about your HC. Now, the conscious mind will continually focus on the faith, attaching a feeling/emotion to it (faith) and store it in the subconscious mind as our HC behavior, habit, belief of our HC.

For example -

If you are constantly worried about money and think that it is very difficult to be rich in the PS, the conscious mind will continually focus on the non-HC thoughts regarding Money, attaching emotion to it and storing it in the subconscious mind as a non-HC belief about Money. It may stop us from becoming RICH.

But, if we set MONEY in our HC and have the Aim and Purpose for it, we will constantly follow the HC thoughts about money and think of becoming rich. So, the conscious mind will continually focus on the FAITH, attaching a feeling/emotion of FAITH to it and storing it in the subconscious mind as an HC belief about Money. Thus, we shall be rich in the RS and with abundance in the SS.

In the PS, we prepare our SC mind to have great HC beliefs and habits by following the HC thoughts about our HC, i.e., about our Aim, Money and Purpose while also preparing our Aim, a mindset for Money and a great emotion for our Purpose. The subconscious does not see any difference between an HC thought or a non-HC thought.

The thoughts of the conscious mind, the ones which we repeat (by chanting), hold for the longest, enjoy, whether consciously or unconsciously, the subconscious mind takes as true and stores them as Belief. (Chanting is when we are thinking the HC thoughts of our HC consciously, so we avoid the non-HC thoughts which we may be chanting unconsciously.)

So, the best thing is to start chanting the HC thoughts related to our HC, and thus have them stored in our mind as an HC belief.

Knowing how the mind works helps us know clearly how important it is to become aware and conscious of our thoughts, mainly the HC thoughts.

Our HC gives us focused, specific, and conscious HC thoughts, and produces focused, specific, and conscious thoughts and things which help us reach the RS and the SS. These are the HC thoughts and the HC things that we want for our life.

When we become purposefully conscious (aware) of our HC thoughts, we know how important the HC thoughts are in the RS. The HC thoughts that we think about on a daily basis continually create our beliefs and habits for our HC.

We need to be just a little educated so as to understand the difference between HC thoughts and feelings and the the non-HC thoughts and feelings, and that it creates beliefs and habits for our HC in the RS. Set a big HC.

Our subconscious mind doesn't differentiate between big or small either. Now, our work is to follow the HC thoughts, chanting for our big HC in the PS with FAITH. We don't need to think about anything else in the PS because we have something in the RS and the SS that will take care of our big HC.

Just prepare your HC in the PS with FAITH. Avoid limiting beliefs and the non-HC thoughts and things in your life every day. We all were born FREE.

We all have FREE that can give us our BIG HC.

We all have FREE, not 1 or 2 in a million persons, but all of us 7.4+ billion people.

2. SC Mind (Subconscious Mind)

As we become mature by the age of 30–40, our subconscious comes into action or becomes active. We start to understand the SC Mind well during this age, i.e., in the RS. The SC Mind is harmonious because it is linked with the SUPREME. When we are young in the PS, we cannot understand the SC Mind too well. When we are young, we should realize our finite mind (the thinking part of the mind) by following/chanting HC thoughts in the finite mind. In this way, we make our SC Mind harmonious for our HC, i.e., Aim, Money and Purpose for the RS. We cannot use our SC Mind like our finite mind, but we can make it more and more harmonious every day.

The SC mind has 7-8 things one needs to know -

1. It stores the HC thoughts and feelings we enjoyed, repeated (chanted) and held by the conscious mind in the PS (14–30 years of age). These HC thoughts will become creative in the RS.

2. The HC thoughts and feelings we enjoyed, repeated (chanted) and held by the conscious mind in the PS (14–30 years of age) form HC beliefs based on those thoughts and feelings in the SC Mind. We will have those HC beliefs and habits during the RS (30–40 years of age).

3. The SC Mind does not see any difference between an HC thought and a non-HC thought.

4. The SC Mind has bondage, Question/Worry/Fear/Doubt (Q,W,F,D), creating unnecessary (Q/W/F/D).

5. The SC Mind does not think of the finite mind, so it does not have thoughts like the finite mind. So, it is also the no-thought part of the mind.

6. The SC Mind likes the deepest HC thoughts, plans, and IDEAS. We have the U/aim (purpose) in our HC, so the HC thoughts become the deepest.

7. The SC Mind works automatically, e.g., our breath and heartbeat is controlled by the SC Mind. We all know we don't make any effort in breathing or in the beating of the heart, its automatic. The SC Mind works EFFORTLESSLY in its way of doing things.

8. The SC Mind also has a connection with the SUPREME, so the SC Mind likes, knows and helps us in our Purpose.

Points 1, 2, 3, 4, we will know in the PS (14–30 years of age).

Points 5, 6, 7, 8, we will know in the RS (30–40 years of age).

1. It stores thoughts and feelings we enjoyed, repeated (chanted) and held by the conscious mind in the PS (14–30 years of age). The SC mind does not think, but stores what we have conceived by a free mind. The SC Mind does not know thoughts, but only the feelings. When we choose the HC thoughts and mix them with FAITH, the HC thoughts turn into HC feelings, and the SC Mind then knows it and stores it. The HC thoughts which we chanted (repeated), enjoyed, held consciously for the longest time, the subconscious mind takes them as true and stores them upon being given by the conscious mind.

2. Our role is to follow the great HC thoughts, high moral values and principals, abundant beliefs and read great books (Reading great books is one of the best ways to have great HC thoughts and feelings), so that we make our SC Mind the best in the RS (30–40 years of age). Thus, our HC beliefs (caused by our HC thoughts and feelings mixed with FAITH), behavior and habits are created. Beliefs have the HC thoughts, our obsessions, our ideals, ideas, values, and our FAITH in the SUPREME.

3. The subconscious mind does not see any difference between an HC thought and a non-HC thought. The SC Mind has no power to distinguish if something is an HC thought or a non-HC thought. The thoughts which we repeat (by chanting), held the longest, and enjoyed the most, whether consciously or unconsciously, the subconscious mind takes as true and stores them upon being given by the conscious mind. So, we should follow the HC thoughts only. The

SC Mind can be given rich feelings (or the HC feelings) because the SC Mind cant tell real from imaginary. It only knows *how* we are feeling. For example–Even though we are not RICH, we should hold the feeling, the habits, the beliefs of being rich to the SC Mind in the PS. The SC Mind would then get an impression of being rich and we shall succeed in telling the SC Mind that we want to be rich and have riches. The SC Mind then takes it as true and makes our RS very EASY.

RICHES = Money, health, happiness, harmonious relationships, a harmonious life.

4. The SC Mind has bondage, questions/worry/fear/doubt(Q/W/F/D). The SC mind creates unnecessary (Q/W/F/D). Sometimes, bondage is good when it stops us from following the non-HC thoughts and doing non-HC things. For example, when we want to do something non-HC or not a good thing, the bondage in our SC Mind will warn us; that is the wonderful part of the SC Mind bondage. But the other kind of bondage creates bondage for our HC. The moment we set our HC, the first thought will come to our mind, 'Oh, I can't get it,' or 'Oh, it's not possible. I can't be rich, it's hard, I am not lucky.' Know that it is the bondage of the SC Mind that is speaking this. Our job is to go ahead while overcoming the bondage. Because it is the nature of the SC Mind to create bondage for our HC, our nature is to move ahead by overcoming it and keep preparing our Aim/HC. It is the nature of the SC Mind to have this bondage in the form of worry, doubt, fear and question. 90% of the bondage is created by the SC mind, inwardly, while the outside bondage is only 10%. The outside bondage can be explained as when we listen, see, or experience something not favourable, or encounter some failures. Then we have bondage and think that we can't be rich, etc., or we can't

have our HC. It's mainly the inside bondage because of which many of us don't even set an HC. By faith, we overcome the 90% inside bondage in the PS (14–30 years of age), and by knowing the YOU/FREE in the RS (30–40 years of age), the rest of the 10% will be overcome.

Take the bondage of the SC Mind as a means to check our FAITH. Bondage of the SC Mind does not stop us, but is there for us to grow our FAITH. Never think of ending/controlling the bondage, but to overcome it, as it is the nature of the SC Mind. It never stops us from going ahead with our HC, but makes us stronger with our FAITH in hard times. It keeps us awake to move towards the RS (30–40 years of age) with FAITH. Time to time in the PS (14–30 years of age), we will have bondage from the SC Mind, but just know that it is the SC Mind that is causing the bondage and checking the FAITH in our HC. Just overcome it with FAITH and keep preparing your Aim/HC. Your part is to overcome it by following/chanting the HC thoughts with FAITH.

Make great beliefs in the SC Mind by chanting the HC thoughts with FAITH in the PS, overcome the BONDAGE of the SC Mind with FAITH in the PS and finally by starting to use the SC Mind, we enter in the RS. Our conscious mind allows us to decide what we want, while our SC Mind just wants to know what we want, i.e., Let the SC Mind know what our HC is.

So, we set the HC and write it to tell it to our SC Mind. Most of us are not RICH, but the HC thoughts make our SC Mind feel the RICHES. Following/Chanting the HC thoughts change the blueprint of our SC Mind in the PS. The SC Mind does not engage in the process of proving what is an HC or a non-HC thought.

The sure method of overcoming the non-HC thoughts is by following/chanting the HC thoughts by repeating, enjoying, holding, which then the SC Mind accepts as TRUE, thus eventually forming new and healthy HC beliefs, behavior and habits.

The SC Mind is the seat of Habit also. At least ninety percent of our mental life is subconscious. The SC Mind is not only the result of heredity, but the result of home, business and the social environment where countless impressions, ideas and thoughts are received. Much of this is received from others, the result of opinions, suggestions or statements. A major part of it is the result of our own thinking, but nearly all of it has been accepted with little or no examination or consideration. The conscious mind receives it, passes it on to the subconscious, where it is taken up and becomes a habit. So, we should allow only the HC thoughts in. See, listen, speak the HC, HC thoughts and HC related things. The functional mind is the teacher of the SC Mind (the student) in the PS (14–30 years of age). If the teacher teaches HC thoughts and feelings to the student (SC Mind), the latter will then have HC beliefs, behavior and habits in the RS (30–40 years of age). These HC thoughts and feelings which the functional mind repeated, held and enjoyed will be the HC beliefs, habits and knowledge of the SC mind in the RS (30–40 years of age). By repeating HC thoughts day after day with FAITH, our SC Mind is made to act on them and takes them true. In this way, the HC beliefs, habits, behavior and knowledge are formed. These HC thoughts go deep into our SC Mind and make the corresponding HC beliefs, habits, behavior and knowledge.

The SC Mind displays these HC thoughts and feelings in the RS (30–40 years of age). It will be beneficial to know YOU/FREE because we need the SC Mind in the RS (30–40 years of age); so we should focus only on the HC thoughts so that the SC Mind is ready in the RS. Later, the SC Mind would take us to the SS (40+–80+ years of age) smoothly. The SC Mind receives the thoughts and ideas unto itself through the feelings our HC has. Excellent HC thoughts have great HC feelings that work to grow our Sub-Conscious Mind to reach the RS (30–40 years of age), and it will help us to know YOU/FREE in the RS.

Free will play the RESULTS part for our HC.

All the PS heads which we are following are to impress the SC Mind, and we are following the PS (14–30 years of age) schedule to reach the RS (30–40 years of age).

We are ready now to begin our PS (14–30 years of age) for preparing our HC mainly or the Aim.

The PS has 6 heads:

1.Faith

2.HC thoughts chanting

3.Brahamacharya

4.Constant practice

1.Visualization, and

2.Time Table

2

The Preparing Schedule (14–30 years of age)

HC level 1/Free level 1

The PS prepares for HC and HC related things: H, H, HR, HL (health, happiness, harmonious relationships and a harmonious life), as well as our studies/job. So vast is the range of the PS.

As we (our senses) come in contact with objects, we beget desires, desires bring thoughts, and thus the thoughts/ desires overtake our FREE. It disconnects us from the billions and the Supreme, and the fullness of our gratitude goes down.

1. From the fullness of Gratitude, we have come down to FAITH (faith is born of Gratitude).

2. From oneness with the billions and the Supreme, we have come to Mind and EGO.

3.From being FREE from all, we have come down to thoughts and desires.

It means that we were at FREE level 3 and HC level 3.As we started having desires, we came down the FREE level schedules. We may again get our FREE level 3 and HC level 3, as well as our HC.

There are 5 schedules in our life -

1. The Supreme schedule (The SS: 0- **14** years of age)–Free, one with the Supreme, full of Gratitude–FREE level 3 / HC level 3

2. The Preparing schedule (The PS: **14** -30 years of age)–Mainly about **Aim**/Preparing our HC–FREE level 1 / HC level 1

3. The Receiving schedule (The RS: 30-40 years of age)–Mainly about the Knowledge of FREE **and getting READY for RESULTS**, HC–FREE level 2 / HC level 2

4. The Supreme schedule (The SS:40+-till last 80+)–Mainly about **RECEIVING** our HC/RESULTS & FREE level 4,HC–FREE level3 / HC level 3

5. The POS schedule (Afterlife, i.e., after 80)–All HC complete and FREE level 4

HC level is related to our HC, the Outside things, i.e., preparing the HC, having skills and specialized knowledge about our HC, while the FREE level is related to FREE, the Inside things, i.e., knowing the Mind, YOU/FREE, the billions, the Supreme,the Gratitude, and the Surrender.

We need to grow together with the HC level 1 and the FREE level 1.

The **Purpose**, faith grows the FREE level 1. That's why we have **Purpose** for Free level 1.

Along with HC level 1, we have FREE level 1 too, and we need to grow them together. We do well in the PS when both the FREE level and the HC level increase together, i.e., Inside and Outside.

Our HC has the **Purpose**, while the PS has FAITH to grow the FREE level. Our thoughts then break all boundaries and the mind goes beyond its limitations.

Action alone is our province, not the RESULTS.

Just focus on preparing our HC in the PS. In reality, we don't need to think about RESULTS either; FREE works for our RESULTS.

Later when we discuss FREE in the book, we will understand.

Our HC as well as M, H, H, HR, HL come to you themselves when YOU become FREE.

In the PS, preparing is not very difficult; the most challenging part is the RESULTS that FREE plays for YOU, so be easy. Results include receiving, sustaining, maintaining, completing, and all complete our HC, FREE does it all.

We don't need to worry about success or failure, pleasure or pain, happiness or sadness due to our temporary shortcomings in preparing our HC by our effort in the PS (14–30 years of age), no need at all,because there is Action alone in the PS(14–30 years of age).

The PS given to us is capable of preparing for even the most significant HC. We can follow the PS along with our studies and job. The PS applies to our studies or job as well. The PS is there for preparing our highest HC. It also prepares for us to gain health, happiness, a harmonious life, and harmonious relationships.

The PS is for the YOUNGSTERS (14–30 years of age) who have set their HC. Understand again that we give in more or less the same effort for a low HC. So why not set the highest HC, when the effort is more or less the same and write the HC in your dairy.

Do not hesitate. Write down the highest HC.

The PS schedule is headed by FAITH and has 6 heads.

The 6 heads are as given below:-

1. Faith:

After waking up in the morning and before sleeping at night, follow the Faith prayer in the PS.

2.HC thoughts chanting:

Daily chanting of the HC thoughts in your mind.

3. Brahamcharya:

4. Constant Practice: Practice for your Aim constantly

5. Visualization of HC

6. TIME – A timetable

During a young age, we follow these heads of the PS (14–30 years of age).

All the heads of the PS, individually and altogether, accumulate FAITH in our HC and the Faith in our minds. The six heads are headed by FAITH. The PS lasts till 30 years of age, so we should follow all the heads steadily. It takes time to accumulate Faith, to grow from our HC level 1 and Free level 1, and it takes time to prepare for our AIM.

PS (14–30 years of age) is the foundation. If the foundation is solid, all life will be celebrated. Let's say we have an average life of 80+, so we shall need M, H, H, HR, HL (Money, health, happiness, harmonious relationships and a harmonious life) till the very end. PS (14–30 years of age) will prepare for us a solid foundation of M, H, H, HR, HL till the end (i.e., 80+).

This foundation would keep us stay with M, H, H, HR, HL in the RS (30–40 years of age) and give us an abundance of M, H, H, HR, HL in the SS (40+–80+). In the PS, our mind is curious to know the RS and the SS, but one must have Faith in the HC and in the SUPREME. In time, we shall know all and will surely reach there harmoniously. It is now time to enjoy our PS.

This is your book; you may write on the pages and thus have a record.

1. Faith

We need Faith to grow and prepare our HC.

Never use Faith for results; FREE plays the RESULTS part for our life.

Have and keep FAITH only for preparing our HC level 1 and FREE level 1. For results, we have FREE. Faith believes that is beyond the power of reason.

- Mahatma Gandhi

Faith is not something to grasp; it is a state to grow into.

Faith will lead you to the RS. Repetition of affirmation is the only way to grow the emotion of Faith. The emotions or the 'feeling' part of thoughts give thoughts life and action.

The emotions of Faith mixed with the HC thoughts provide greater action. Have Faith in your HC, in your HC thoughts, in your beliefs (according to your religion or belief), and it will take us to the RS.

We have a great HC, to have Money by a great Aim and to use the Money for a greater purpose.

Have faith in the SUPREME (according to your religion or belief) whether you're religious, an atheist or non-religious.

Have belief in YOU and an in-depth heartfelt look into YOURSELF, and whether it matches with the SUPREME.

Whenever we feel uneasy in the PS, know that the mind is thinking about the RESULTS, know that Action alone is our province, not the RESULTS; FREE plays the RESULTS part of our HC.

The essence of the PS is to prepare our HC (main aim) with FAITH. Faith is related to the SUPREME; it grows our Faith in Mind, YOU and the billions. We need not know about the SUPREME in the PS, just have faith in the SUPREME.

We will know the Supreme in the RS, so have faith in the SUPREME in the PS. With all the faith in our HC, we pray to the Supreme **for preparing our HC**.

The Main FAITH Prayer:

Please help us in preparing us our HC.

Please help us by following the HC thoughts.

Please help us in following Good values and principles, and harmonious relationships.

Please help us in following Brahamcharya for great morals, good health and wealth.

Please help us for preparing our PS.

Please forgive our mistakes.

In the FAITH prayer, we may add, while giving thanks for preparing your HC, no need to ask for RESULTS in the prayer because gratitude is beyond demands. Give thanks for preparing the HC in advance. Have great feelings for your HC and have FAITH in your HC.

We have set a high Harmonious Combination, i.e., having MONEY by having a great AIM and using the MONEY for our Ultimate AIM too. It is your Faith in your HC that is going to take you to the RS.

During the PS, we accumulate FAITH in our HC along with the practice for our aim. It is the Faith in our HC that makes us follow the other five heads every day. And then, all the heads together and individually accumulate the Faith in the HC.

Follow the Faith prayer every day (after waking up in the morning, after waking up (a/w) in the morning and before sleeping (b/s) at night) with faith in your Aim of the HC and with a great feeling in our HC. Thus, we get thoughts related to our HC, which we should follow/chant in our mind. There are times when we have temporary failures and we lose some faith in the HC and the PS.

Keep following the Faith prayer every day, having faith in your HC. We will bounce back with double the Faith in our HC. The daily Faith prayer and having Faith in our HC give our mind the harmonious feeling of our HARMONIOUS COMBINATION (Aim – Money – Ultimate Aim).

Have faith in the idea, i.e., Action alone is our province, not the RESULTS; FREE plays the RESULTS part for our HC.

One idea can change your life. **Have faith in the truth of the HC thoughts.**

With each passing day, we come across new HC thoughts and HC things. So, by living each day in Faith, exercising it and growing it, our faith is strengthened through adversity. Read good books by enlightened people; it will strengthen us when we are weak. Their faith will give us Faith and courage.

'Faith' is having total trust in something or someone mainly in the SUPREME. Faith is a spiritual force, a deep love and trust in the Supreme and yourself. Faith is a state of mind that grows by the confirmations and affirmations of truth. Give affirmations to yourself regularly about the aim you want to prepare, and have the positive self-talk with yourself. It helps to grow our Faith. Believe only in the positive suggestions you have about yourself.

The HC thoughts you repeatedly confess to yourself are all that matter. Believing in yourself along with constant positive HC affirmations to your mind which will grow your Faith. This is how we develop our Faith.

The mind is very simple, whatever you suggest to it repeatedly, over and over again, it will take as the Truth. Read good books; as you read the greats and their values and principles, you will find the same faith to match in yourself. It will grow and establish your Faith. (We were born free, one with the billions and the SUPREME, and full of Gratitude -Faith is born of gratitude, we already have it). We need to grow it in the PS, so it would become Gratitude in the RS; this is called growing the Free level 1 (Faith) to Free level 2 (Gratitude).

Preparing our Aim of HC with Faith in the PS would become a VALUE (regarding MONEY) in the RS; this is called growing of the HC level 1 (Preparing) to HC level 2 (VALUE regarding MONEY).

Liberate your faith through prayer, Faith prayer, saying thanks for preparing our HC, our values, and for preparing all the heads of the PS. Faith is the heads of the PS and Faith itself guides us to develop our HC level 1 and FREE level 1. Have FAITH in your belief because FAITH will be with us only in the PS (till 30 years of age). Have FAITH in your belief, in your ideas and moral principals, that they will guide you to prepare your HC level 1 and FREE level 1. All the 6 heads have very harmonious thoughts which accumulate Faith in our HC.

2.HC Thought Chanting

HC thoughts are related to our HC, i.e. Aim, Money and Purpose, as well as HC related things such as health, happiness, harmonious relationships and a harmonious life (h, h, hr, hl).Plus, they cover all the areas of thoughts about Brahamcharya, visualization, timetable, practice, values, principles, ideals, etc. Most of us billions are not rich and need to grow our HC level and FREE level. The only way to do so is by following the HC thoughts.

It rewrites the SC Mind's beliefs, habits, and behavior. It overcomes the Bondage. It opens up the limited beliefs. Be careful about choosing your thoughts. Always choose the HC thoughts and mix them with Faith, so the SC Mind stores them. It is our thoughts only which either upgrade us or degrade us. The HC thoughts improve us, while the non-HC thoughts degrade us. The choice is ours. Always choose the HC thoughts because most of us billions are not rich and need to grow. We should not hold/follow the non-HC thoughts, e.g., the poverty in our mind. It may lead us to poverty, and we will not be able to grow our HC level and FREE level. Hold the HC thoughts of your HC, riches (h, h, hr, hl are riches) and wealth (cash money + all valuable assets) in your mind, and it will lead you to have riches and wealth (h, h, hr, hl, M ++). Our minds should have the HC and HC related things as our dominating HC thoughts. Both poverty and riches are born out of thought. There is no secret about them, we all understand them. Thoughts have energy. HC thoughts are powerful because they are based on the HC, i.e., Aim–Money–Purpose. We can create thought, so we create the HC thoughts by ourselves. All that we are is what we have thought. What we think, we become. Be very careful of choosing your thoughts, have the HC thoughts so that your SC Mind has good feelings and experiences.

Read the quotes of the greats, the 'thought of the day' written on your school/college chalkboard. (I used to read and follow the thought of the day for that day or week, and then a new thought became the thought of the day in my mind.) Know that active HC thought chanting is till PS only. In the PS, the thoughts of results would come, but don't let your success or failure make you uneasy. Keep going with your HC, whether in success or failure, because of Action alone.

In PS, the HC thoughts are our dominating thoughts, rest all other thoughts are secondary. HC thoughts have HC feelings which go to our SC Mind. If we have HC thoughts, all other non-HC thoughts become weak.

The HC thoughts which we put on top, the ones we keep or hold, repeat and enjoy the most in the PS go to the SC Mind. So, always have HC thoughts as your dominating thoughts to keep/hold, repeat and enjoy in the PS (till 30 years of age), because thoughts are only in the PS. In the RS, we will have a different schedule. The role of F.Mind actively ends in the PS.

HC thoughts have HC feelings about our HC, so only the HC feelings enter the SC Mind. In the PS, don't try to control the F Mind, make it your friend, thank it for having HC thoughts.

What are your main HC thoughts in the PS? Write them down . In the PS, we can't stop the non-HC thoughts, but we can have the HC thoughts as the dominating thoughts. Thus, we make the non-HC thoughts secondary. Writing is important. Write in this book space , so that you may check where you are and what HC thoughts you are following/ chanting.

By writing these on one side of the page, you can track the HC thoughts you are following in the PS.

HC chanting is a powerful way to be with your HC. It's a form of a Mantra. It's a way to keep yourself with your HC and keep away the non-HC thoughts.

It shows your commitment to your HC too. Always chant the HC thoughts in a phrase or a small sentence. Ideas should be read; we are often not able to chant ideas because they are in the form of a big sentence. The Finite Mind has thoughts, feelings, imagination, willpower, and determination.

One of the biggest achievements of the PS is to chant HC thoughts of the HC. In this way, we prepare our HC in our minds, as well as overcome the non-HC thoughts and the bondage of the SC Mind (Q/W/F/D) by chanting HC thoughts with FAITH.

HC thoughts chanting in the mind:

DAILY CHANTING THE HC THOUGHTS IN THE MIND –

This head is the only head in the PS which we follow with extra effort for our highest HC.

We understand all the other heads of the PS that are:

1.FAITH

3.Brahamcharya

4.Constant practice of Aim

5.Visualization of HC

6. Timetable

But, HC thoughts chanting is the extra effort required for our biggest HC. This head makes the difference between a low HC and the highest HC. Those who have set a low HC usually follow the other 5 heads except this head. But those who have set the highest HC should follow this head along with the other five heads. As we set our HIGHEST HC and come with FAITH in it every day, we get thoughts related to our HC in our mind.

We should follow these HC thoughts and chant them in our mind, and constantly act on these thoughts too.

By CHANTING HC related thoughts in our Mind:

a. We accumulate FAITH in our HC.

b. We hold our HC in our mind.

c. We do not allow the non–HC thoughts to come to our mind.

d. We observe our FINITE MIND (the thinking part of the mind) and consciously use our FINITE MIND for our HC.

e. We understand the difference between the Finite mind (the thinking part of the mind) and the SC Mind (the non-thinking part of Mind).

a. By chanting the HC related thoughts in our mind, we accumulate Faith in our HC.

By Faith prayer, as we get HC related thoughts in our mind, we should chant them in our mind and should constantly act on them. We will find them giving us good feelings, and help and motivate us to practice for our Aim. Thus comes the Faith in our HC related thoughts as we keep chanting and repeating them. Many HC related thoughts come to our mind and we keep following and chanting them in the PS. We get non–HC thoughts also. Keep CHANTING HC thoughts, that is the only solution to overcome the non-HC thoughts.

During our youth, our FINITE MIND is very active. We should take full advantage of it by following the HC thoughts. Only these HC thoughts and feelings of the HC are going to become the great HC beliefs, HC habits and give a secure understanding of reaching the RS. HC related thoughts are HC thoughts.

b. By chanting the HC related thoughts in our mind, we hold our HC in our mind. In our Finite mind (the thinking part of mind), millions of thoughts come and go. By chanting the HC related thoughts in our mind, we hold our HC in our mind. This is very important. We should only allow our HC related thoughts to come into our mind. By chanting the HC related thoughts in our mind, we hold our HC in our mind. Thus, we do not allow the non-HC and the non-HC thoughts in our mind and and keep our HC in it.

c. By chanting the HC related thoughts in our mind, we do not allow the non-HC thoughts to come to our mind. The non-HC thoughts are always ready to enter into our mind. Our HC has everything in it; HC as well as health, happiness, harmonious relationships and a harmonious life, thoughts and things. So, we do not need any non-HC thoughts to come into our mind or to stay there.

d. By chanting the HC related thoughts in our mind, we observe our FINITE MIND (the thinking part of the mind) and use our FINITE MIND for our HC, consciously. To go in the RS, we should understand our FINITE MIND. By chanting the HC related thoughts in our mind, we observe how the Finite Mind works. We observe how thoughts come and go in our FINITE MIND. It is difficult to stop the non-HC thoughts from coming into our FINITE MIND.

But, by chanting the HC thoughts, we learn to overcome the non-HC thoughts to come and stay in our FINITE MIND. By chanting the HC related thoughts in our finite mind, we use our finite mind (the thinking part of the mind) for our HC related thoughts.

e. To know the difference between the Finite mind and the SC Mind

When we know the difference between the Finite mind and the SC mind, we may understand the FREE.

If we don't use our FINITE MIND for HC thoughts, then our F mind may go for non-HC thoughts. If then we start following the non-HC thoughts, consciously or unconsciously, we store the non-HC thoughts in our SC Mind.

But, if we use our FINITE MIND for HC related thoughts only, consciously by chanting them, we make a conscious effort to reach the RS. Every day, a thought related to the HC and from the heads of the PS comes into our FINITE MIND. That thought should become the thought of the day and we should follow it by chanting it in our mind. That thought may even last for 3-4 days. We test and experiment with it to prepare our Aim and the HC.

When we find it useful, we keep repeating it in our mind until it becomes secure there. Then, another thought comes and so on through all of the PS.

Now we understand the F Mind by chanting the HC thoughts and know how the F mind works.

If we chant the HC thoughts, we will understand the SC Mind well. Thus, we will also know what the difference is between the thinking part of the mind (the Finite Mind) and the non-thinking part of the mind (the SC Mind). Otherwise, the F Mind and the SC Mind will appear the same.

Chanting is a way to focus your mind; it is the 1st stage or a simple form of meditation. We will feel easy by following/chanting the HC thoughts, while the non-HC thoughts make us uneasy. HC thoughts chanting shows our commitment to the HC and the PS (Free level 1 / HC desire level 1).

We use HC thoughts as affirmations continuously and as often during the day as possible, and continue to do so until they become a part of us as a form of habit. Mental strength is gained in precisely the same way that physical strength is secured, by exercise.

In the beginning, the HC thoughts chanting might seem a little difficult, but it gradually becomes easier and develops into a mental habit. Finally, it becomes automatic. We then become positive of what we think; there is no doubt about it any longer.

You may not succeed the first time you try, but to overcome the non-HC thoughts, you should follow/chant the HC thoughts because only they can lead you to the RS from HC level 1 / Free level 1 to HC level 2 / Free level 2.

Chanting involves repeating the words or small sentences related to our HC in order to focus and clear our mind to prepare our HC. By chanting the HC thoughts related things over and over, our SC Mind will be made to believe it and take it as true.

It can be done for some hours during the day, with gaps for rest and adjusted according to capacity. No proper position or place is required for it. Never overdo it; do it in a relaxed and easy way. We can even chant while eating. We can keep chanting while doing other activities.

When chanting is continuous, we are continuously in an 'awakened state', i.e., in a continuous state of meditation. Chanting gives us a spiritual experience. Through chanting, we attain a natural state of communion with our faith.

A protective shield is formed around us when we chant that wards off non-HC thoughts.

We usually chant many thoughts unconsciously, so it would be better to chant some HC thoughts consciously.

The practice of chanting has been around for over 5,000 years and is defined as the continuous recitation of mantras in India.

A mantra is a Sanskrit word meaning, in rough translation, "to deliver the mind".

Make the HC thought chanting short and simple. Use a phrase or at most a sentence. You may repeat it over and over again. Always affirm the Faith. Make your affirmation a positive statement.

Don't force yourself to believe it, just chant it; the SC Mind would believe it. All we have to do is to repeat it over and over again, and the affirmation will quite naturally affect the mind.

Make the HC thought simple and easy to chant. Never over-do the chanting.

Replace your non-HC self-talk/non-HC thought with an HC thought.

Change your non-HC language to HC language; from “I can’t do this” to “I can do this”;from “I can’t be rich” to “I can be rich”.

When we select an HC thought to chant and repeat, we are affirming it to ourselves and allow its meaning to seep into our SC Mind, helping to shift our non-HC beliefs, habits and behavior patterns to HC ones.

When HC thoughts become the main thoughts, we permit them to occupy our mind. When someone in our family is going to get married, how carefully we choose everything; it is the same for our HC. We should choose the HC thoughts, which are to remain for our lives till the very end.

HC thoughts are a counter measure to check the non-HC thoughts as well, which we follow unconsciously.

For example, if we place a non-HC thought that it is difficult to be rich or watch things that are related to not being rich ,the counter measure would be to place the HC thoughts in the Functional Mind, so we grow a strong belief to be rich and get our aim and the HC.

Don’t think of the RESULTS in the PS. We don’t need to think about the RESULTS at all; just focus on preparing our Aim for the HC in the PS.

Use your MIND for preparing the HC, i.e., the AIM, MONEY, and PURPOSE in the PS.

Action alone is thy province, not the results.

Free plays the RESULTS part. I concluded that from the great book 'Bhagavad Gita'. This is the biggest IDEA and the baseline of this book.

The Bhagavad Gita, the 5000 years old book, and its messages are so true and relevant even today.

We are in a better position in the way of living by following our PS.

3. Brahamcharya

To him who is disciplined in food and recreation, puts an effort in all activities, and in sleep and waking, yoga (discipline) becomes a relief from all ills.

– Bhagavad Gita

Brahmacharya (usually translated as 'celibacy') *means not only the sexual continence, but involves the observance of all the cardinal vows for the attainment of Brahman.*

- Bhagavad Gita

Tranquil in spirit, free from fear, steadfast in the vows of Brahmacharya, holding his mind in control, the yogi should sit with all his thoughts on me, absorbed in me.

- Bhagavad Gita

Brahmacharya - the highest behavior in thoughts, words, and deeds.

Brahm + acharan makes up the word Brahmacharya.

Braham – Supreme, Acharan – Conduct.

That is what Brahmacharya means- Supreme Conduct.

Brahmacharya is an important head of the PS, that helps in preparing our Aim/HC very much and leads us from the PS to the RS. Brahmacharya is the discipline of thought, word, action and sexual activity.

One of the main practices of Brahmacharya is the practice of celibacy in thought, word, and deed. It translates to a disciplining of sexual activities, but also the disciplining of all the senses in thought, word, and deed.

Sexual desire is one of the strongest desires. We should discipline and organize it. Never control but discipline and organize your sex-related activities. Brahmacharya is the energy which gives us the mental and physical strength to prepare our PS.

By the practice of Brahmacharya, one is granted longevity, glory, strength, vigor, knowledge, physical charm, wealth, undying fame, virtues and devotion, and also a growth in the FREE level 1 / HC level 1.

For the knowledge of YOU/FREE in the RS, we should follow and establish Brahmacharya well in the PS. We need to follow the truth (moral principles and values) for FREE level 1 / HC desire level 1 in the PS to prepare our HC and to reach HC level 2 / Free level 2 in the RS.

We need power and discipline to follow Brahmacharya. Will-power is using the finite mind to follow the HC thoughts of Brahmacharya.

Respect for elders, purity, rectitude, continence, and harmlessness–all this is physical austerity. Speech that hurts no one, is true, pleasant to listen to and beneficial, and constantly studies the scriptures–this is the austerity in speech. Serenity, kindness, silence, self-control and purity–this is the austerity of the mind. Make some moral principles and follow them in the PS.

Nonviolence is the weapon of the strong. Forgiveness is the attribute of the strong. Strength does not come from physical capacity, it comes from a strong will. Always be at complete harmony of thought, word and deed. Always try purifying your thoughts.

When in doubt, it's better to keep quiet/silent than to speak. Be able to maintain your own highest standards of moral principals. Being Non-violent, truthful, dedicated, committed, avoiding greed, lust, wrath, having the purity of heart, steadfastness in knowledge and action, beneficence, self-restraint, sacrifice, practicing spiritual study, austerity, uprightness, gentleness, modesty, forgiveness, fortitude, making a respectful bow to the Supreme are the values to grow in oneself.

Brahmacharya makes our BODY and MIND strong, healthy as well as groomed. It develops our personality. Our HC and the PS are great to make us organized and disciplined. We should follow our HC with determination. Our HC wants us to be strong both in body and mind. We have set the highest HC. We should develop our personality for our HC as well.

Follow good morals in life. Study good literature. We have the faith, determination and will-power to follow the HC. By resolution, we can organize and discipline our sexual activities. It makes our mind and body healthy and strong for our HC and the Aim of our HC in the PS. Our faith, determination and will-power are our refuge. Faith in the HC, keeping/chanting the HC related thoughts in our mind, constantly practicing the aim, visualization of the HC and the caring time keep us organized and disciplined.

Have a circle of good friends. Keep doing regular exercise of the body by taking part in a sports activity. Indulge in recreational activities. Study the biographies of the greats. Eat healthy food. Respect your parents, elders, and teachers. Talk to them with respect. Listen to them well and obey them. Take care of the younger ones.

You have been given the PS to follow to be organized and disciplined. Start every day by following the Faith prayer and having Faith in your HC. Follow the HC related thoughts in your mind. Study WELL.

Do not hurry. Read good books by the greats, as well as the religious books.

Mine is Bhagavad Gita.

It's a book which, when read, remains with one till the very end.

Some of the other books which I have studied a little or more are:

The VEDAS–Vedas are the oldest books in the library of man.

The essence of the Vedas–Learn to discriminate between the permanent and the temporary. Behold the SELF in all beings, SERVE ALL.

UPANISHADS–Upanishads are referred as the last chapters of the Vedas, the highest purpose of the Vedas. Upanishads contain the Hindu philosophical thought.

The essence of Upanishads–Our essential nature is divine. We should behave nobly with compassion, sympathy and love, and should spread happiness everywhere. Don't seek happiness from the outside. Be yourself, turn to the self, the Supreme resides within us, working with us all the time. The self and the Supreme is made of the same substance. Liberation means to be reabsorbed (become one with) into the Supreme. Liberation can be achieved through meditation, introspection and by the knowledge that we are all a part of the whole.

Bhagavad Gita–Essence of Gita–Karma (action), knowledge, surrender.

Karma yoga = action + knowledge; karma yoga is material and spiritual progress.

A Karma yogi dedicates all his physical and mental action to the Supreme.

He self-disciplines himself gradually and becomes FREE.

Some other good books -Think and Grow Rich, The Science of Getting Rich.

Pure air, pure water, wholesome food, physical exercise, outdoor games, walking–all contribute to the maintenance of good health, strength and a high standard of vitality.

There are indeed many ways to gain health and strength. These methods are without a doubt indispensably requisite, but Brahmacharya (celibacy) is the most important of all.

Without Brahmacharya (celibacy), all your exercise is nothing. The Brahmacharya schedule promotes concentration. It disciplines anger.

Mahatma Gandhi was a follower of the constant and careful practice of non-violence, truth, and celibacy. Mahatma Gandhi influenced the world through this power alone.

Through Brahmacharya, we get physical, mental and spiritual advancement in life.

With discipline, we can organize the sexual activities and lust. Lust can be overcome by the mind by having Faith in the PS.

Lust can be overcome by an organized and disciplined Brahmacharya schedule (self-pleasure for youngsters during the PS).

Start a practice of celibacy (self-pleasure),starting weekly in the 1st year and then in 10 days in the 2nd year and so on, to settle between weekly to monthly at the end of the PS.

According to your Brahmacharya schedule(weekly/ monthly), set a day (usually a weekend so that the next day is a holiday), date and time (usually late at night) for self-pleasure (if unmarried; married ones may make love to their partners) and enjoy the activity. Have complete rest for the next day.

Try not to go out, eat a good diet, drink a lot of water and eat fruits. Do the self-pleasure activity only once, knowing that you have to do it the next week too, as per your celibacy schedule.

After self-pleasure, take rest and watch some comedy movie or a comedy show, or listen to a song with good lyrics, enjoy and laugh. Then again, be ready to prepare your Aim of the HC in your PS.

After self-pleasure, the HC thoughts will get reshuffled and new HC thoughts will come. You might think where you are and that is what the blank page in the book is for.

If you write then you may be able to track where you were and then write the new thoughts in it and so on. No need to feel guilty because organized self-pleasure is better than unorganized self-pleasure. Organized self-pleasure schedule checks lust.

Just keep going with the PS. During the process of disciplining celibacy, we should use the energy in preparing our PS. Sex is a need, both for the society and for our own well-being. Abstinence should never be forced, but should be disciplined and organized. Enjoy sex when engaged in it, according to our Brahmacharya schedule.

In fact, when we follow Brahmacharya schedule, you enjoy the sex life more as opposed to being in an unorganized Brahmacharya schedule. A disciplined and organized Brahmacharya brings a healthy relationship to our life and gives great strength and energy to our PS.

Diet is an essential factor for following disciplined celibacy.

Sportspersons and people involved in physical activities may eat non-veg. For the rest of the others, a vegetarian diet is the best for the PS. Have good eating habits. Drink luke-warm water in the morning after getting up.

In the PS, Brahmacharya is important for health, moral values, behavior, discipline and a good sexual life. Simple living and high thinking is a great achievement. So, we should decorate ourselves with the good qualities. Fasting is also a perfect purification exercise; we may do it weekly or monthly by eating only fruits on that day. The PS becomes complete with Brahmacharya.

The discipline process is little difficult. It requires a constant organizing. We should have a regular, righteous, moderate, and disciplined life. Have patience, perseverance, determination and a strong will. Practice the discipline of the senses (see right, speak right and listen right), right conduct, right thinking, right acting and following/chanting the HC thoughts.

Sleep well; we need 8 hours of sleep in a day. Have a nap in the afternoon to have a focused mind. Exercise, or simply walk. Follow the Faith prayer to be thankful for help in following the Brahmacharya for preparing our Aim of our HC. Drink hot water every day, time to time.

Acne is common among youngsters, so avoid dairy, flour and pork products. It will cure the acne.

We may get Vitamins from less expensive foods to strengthen our immune system. Papaya and green leafy vegetables have plenty of vitamin C. Peanuts contain the valuable vitamin E. Bananas have vitamin B-6. Sweet potatoes and carrots have vitamin A.

Practice your aim every day and sleep well. On weekends, have a relaxing time. Relax your body and mind. Take rest from the practice of AIM and the chanting of HC related thoughts in your mind, so that you may start again after the weekend.

With a little more effort and determination, we should keep following our PS. No need to hurry, but be organized and disciplined. This is the only way to follow the highest HC and the PS. We have TIME; 14-16 years.

Do not try to control the mind, rather love, discipline and organize it. The mind can become very powerful with the HC thoughts.

Choose the HC thoughts and give them to your mind.

A clean living, an unceasing concentration on wisdom, regular study of the good books, truth, absence of wrath, presence of courtesy, modesty, forgiveness, fortitude, purity–these are the Good Qualities. Overcome lust, wrath, greed, and ignorance. Eat the foods that prolong life and increase purity, vigor, health, cheerfulness, happiness, and soothing .Make these foods a part of your diet in the PS.

Try to watch comedy, sports and entertainment usually.

Keep this in mind when choosing T.V. shows, movies, and music.

4. Constant Practice

Here, no effort undertaken is lost, no disaster falls. Even a little of this righteous course delivers one from great fear.

– Bhagavad Gita

A slow and steady practice is called 'Constant Practice'. Have great feelings about your HC and constantly practice for your aim every day. Learn the basics to acquire the skills and general knowledge related to your AIM/HC. Constant practice is the only way to learn the basics of specialized skills required for our aim.

Experiment with them. Do not lose heart if one or more experiments fail. Keep practicing and keep learning the skills in the PS.

Hold similar the pleasure and pain, gain and loss, victory and defeat.

–Bhagavad Gita

Undoubtedly, the mind is fickle and hard to curb, yet it can be held in check by constant practice.

– Bhagavad Gita.

Practice 2-4 hours every day for your aim. Along with the practice of your aim, you should constantly practice all the heads of the PS individually and together. In the PS, if we have time, we may do a part-time job or start a small business to form a relation with Money. It depends on our HC.

Again, don't expect results, just do it for preparing or learning the basics and the mindset, as well as to get money and improve your lifestyle, know the value of money, learn about savings, investments, spendings, etc. If it is in your HC, start a part-time or a very small business, not thinking very big if you are not so rich.

Even the rich (below 30 years of age) in the PS should start a small business to flex their muscles on their own. Let it be known however that it is not for the results, but to prepare in the PS, learn the basics and develop a money mindset. In the PS, we constantly act on our Aim and learn the basics of money, i.e., savings and investments.

Even if you have the pocket money of one dollar, try to save a part of it. This habit developed with small amounts will go on similarly with larger amounts too. Get to know about Investments, other sources of Income and the freedom of time. Senses have desires, desires make thoughts, and thoughts lead to action.

Constant practice is an activity to do repeatedly, to improve or to master a skill. "Practice makes one perfect." E.g., Excelling in sports or playing a musical instrument takes a lot of practice. Constant practice is a method of learning and acquiring experience. If we do not practice often enough, we are likely to forget what has been learned.

When we learn a new skill, we are actually changing the mind. We can learn as many new skills in the PS as we want because our mind is like plastic in the PS. We can give it a good shape by learning new skills during this time. Experiment with new skills.

Practicing is simply the only way to get better. Practicing is one of the most rewarding things you will do for yourself. We develop skills through hard work. To get a particular skill for our aim then, we need to practice that skill and repeat it constantly. We have set a big HC, a big aim in it, and the biggest money.

We have much time before 30.Even if we're going to school/college, or have a job, we should constantly practice for our Aim of the HC and make the right habits regarding Money and our Aim.

Always engage in constant practice, never leave it. So wonderful is constant practice. Keep yourself motivated. If your aim is big, you may sometimes be disappointed and want to quit altogether, but know that you are only preparing at this stage.

Remember, your job is ACTION alone and to slowly learn the skill. Develop a practice routine that will get you there. Our actions should match our HC. Balance all activities with practice time. If you want to learn, you will have to give a little extra time to it. Practicing constantly is a necessary action required to make you learn the skills for your aim. We have time. Practice regularly everyday, have ample rest and relax time on weekends to regain energy for the next week.

5. Visualization

Visualization is a form of creative thought by which we make a future from thought and experience. The result of Visualization leads to the development of our Ideal future. Visualization exercise can help gain it. Visualization is a form of creative thought which leads to creative action.

'The true sign of intelligence is not knowledge, but imagination.

Logic will get you from A to B. Imagination will take you everywhere.'

- Albert Einstein

Visualization is a mental technique that uses the imagination. During visualization, we are entirely aware of what we are visualizing and for what. By using only the imagination or visualization, we can change our thoughts and mental images, thus eventually our perception.

If, for example, we are in the PS, we may visualize that we are preparing our aim, money and purpose, and are moving towards the RS. We may even visualize a new skill for our aim. It is one of the easiest but very powerful methods of preparing our HC in the PS. Visualization ends all limitation of the mind. We can visualize beyond our thinking and limits. It allows us to think and see at an infinite level. Such praise for visualization.

To visualize is to see what is not there, but could be there. To visualize is to make visual truths that have a way of coming true. We create images in our mind of our having or doing something about our PS. We repeat these images over and over again. We visualize that we already have our aim, money and u/aim(purpose).

This is a mental trick.

With the visualization technique, we 'live and feel it' as if it is happening to us right now. The subconscious mind cannot distinguish between what is real and what is imagined. Our subconscious will feel the images we create within our mind and store them for the RS, regardless of whether those images reflect our current reality or not. So, through visualization, we prepare our SC Mind along with our conscious mind (Finite Mind) to get more focused HC thoughts.

Visualization works because our mind can't tell the difference between the visualized and the actual event. Since the mind controls the body, it then causes a similar physiological reaction to imaginary experiences as to real experiences. It involves going into a deeply relaxed state and getting specific and clear about our HC, then using our mind to create positive images of something we want to have, or be, and about our HC. Slowly, we become very clear about our HC in our visualization, and all the non-HC things go out of the picture. While during HC chanting, we may sometimes have a non-HC thought, but in visualization, we only have HC things. Visualization is always positive.

Visualization is the conscious creation of our HC in the PS and in moving towards the RS. We purposefully and consciously participate to use the power of visualization to imagine our HC. Visualization is the conscious creation of our HC; we see it, imagine it, feel it as if we already have our HC in real. Practice the visualization techniques on weekends. That day gives rest to the mind and the HC thoughts chanting. Just relax on weekends and follow the practice of visualization.

Visualization balances the PS and generates new HC thoughts, that needs to be done in our HC and the PS. It allows us to relax, replenish and re-energize while keeping the vision alive and well during the PS. That is why visualization is so effective in preparing our subconscious mind for our Aim/HC. Carefully make the mental images which should be consistent. Be clear and create images that are as clear and accurate as possible. Put yourself in the imagination. For example, if you want to be a musician, visualize yourself as playing the music.

Visualization may give us an idea of how the Supreme created all of the universe and the things in the universe similar to his visualization. So, during visualization, we actually come in harmony with the supreme and his way of doing things. We feel that our way is similar to the Supreme's way.

It can put us in a good mood, support us in feeling more confident and getting clearer with what it is that we want to experience our HC, and give our mind the information we want to see in our PS. It is never an activity to be forced to get the HC RESULTS, but only for preparing in the PS. Make it as realistic as possible and have faith in it. Make your visualization practice as pleasant, relaxing, effortless and fun as possible and move ahead for the next week in the PS. By visualizing our HC, we feel we have achieved our HC in advance. This feeling of having our HC strengthens our FAITH in our HC and the PS. We should take time to visualize our HC, visualize that we are going towards money with our aim and purpose. This visualization harmonizes our finite mind and the subconscious mind.

6. Timetable (TT)

A timetable is a time-management tool. It is a list of activities in order, the sequence in which they are intended to take place during the day. Write down what you do every day, including your free time. Make a list of these activities and how much time you spend on them.

Estimate how long you spend commuting to and from school/college, on homework, play, rest, nap, sleep, computer, TV, etc.

TT is like a second clock which indicates all the activities undertaken in a day. It shows the hours of work, kinds of work, rest, recreational time, time of waking up, time of exercising and other such activities. A timetable reflects the entire schedule followed through the day.

A planned TT eliminates the wastage of time and energy. It directs our energy and attention to one thing at a time. By placing a schedule, we do the designated activity properly.

By such a timetable, due attention is given to every time allocated activity. Hourly time is allotted to different activities according to their importance and nature. It helps one develop the Qualities of punctuality and regularity, by placing before the mind a set programme of activities.

It keeps the mind busy, thereby helping in maintaining a regular discipline and ensuring progress too. It also helps to develop the regular habits of work.

A timetable helps in chalking out plans in a systematic manner. **It ensures an equitable distribution of time for different activities, i.e., a balance in work and recreation.** Thus, it has a psychological value leading to the removal of tiredness.

A TT in the PS is the foundation of planning in the RS.

A TT here means a daily or weekly schedule where Mon–Fri is usually the same, but Sat-Sun have some extra relaxing and recreational time added in the TT.

Even in the daily schedule, we should have some relaxed and recreational time. It is not about planning for a month or a year, but the daily schedule for that year.

WakeUp: 5:30/06:00a.m.

Exercise/walk: 06:15-06:30 a.m.

Freshenup/Breakfast: 06:35-7:00a.m.

School/College: 7:00 a.m.–2:00/3:00 p.m.

Rest/Nap: 03:00- 03:30 p.m.

Games: 5:00- 6:00 p.m.

Study: 07:00- 08:00 p.m.

TV /Computer: 08:00-09:00 p.m.

Sleep before: 10 p.m.

Set your TT according to your HC and reset it as you grow up in age and reach the end of the PS. Also, write the TT down on a paper and stick it over your writing desk.

We have 14-16 years for the PS. Follow harmoniously. For these 14-16 years, we should try to follow the PS consciously. We all go through the PS starting from a young age, but only those who have set their HC early and follow the PS consciously become successful.

These 14-16 years will pass by in a great way along with your education (school/college) and job. With all the heads of the PS, we accumulate faith in our HC while preparing our Aim of the HC. With all the FAITH in our HC and after following all the heads of the PS, we come to Faith prayer with great feelings regarding our HC and offer a thanks for receiving help in preparing our HC in the PS, during the 14–30 years of age.

Now we are to enter smoothly into the RS.

We have followed the PS with Faith, HC thought chanting, Brahmacharya, constant practice and TT, along with the ideals, values, and principals in the PS. We have followed the PS consciously (14–30 years of age), while preparing our Aim, a Mindset for Money and the highest emotion with our purpose all together.

We have prepared great HC thoughts and feelings in our HC with Faith. All of these go on to make our RS very easy and become bigger and more simple in the RS and the SS. They become HC IDEAS, BELIEFS, and HABITS in the RS and TRUTH in the SS.

FAITH, mixed with our HC thoughts, Brahmacharya, constant practice, visualization, and TT, take us to the RS and help us then to know YOU/FREE.

Now we are going from the PS to the RS, i.e., from the FREE level 1 / HC level 1 to FREE level 2 / HC level 2.

An overview of the Preparing Schedule (PS) (14- 30 years):

1. Faith 2. Faith in the SUPREME - 3. It grows our Faith in the HC 4. Daily chanting of the HC thoughts in our mind during the day 5. Brahmacharya 6. Constantly practice your Aim 7. Visualization of the HC 8. Time Table	1. Faith prayer 2. Please help us prepare our HC 3. Please give us the HC thoughts , happy relationships ,good health and happiness. 4. Please forgive our mistakes.

HC:

Aim – business, sports, etc.

Money – $

Ultimate Aim – Social responsibility – riches to all

3

The Receiving Schedule (30–40 years of age)

HC level 2 / Free level 2

There is nothing in this world so purifying as Knowledge.

- Bhagavad Gita

It is the man of faith who gains the knowledge; the man who is intent on it and who has mastery over his senses; having acquired the knowledge, he comes here to long the supreme peace.

- Bhagavad Gita

Freedom from pride and pretentiousness, nonviolence, forgiveness, uprightness, service of the Master, purity, stead-fastens, self-restraint;

Aversion from sense-objects, absence of conceit, realization of the painfulness and evil of birth, death, age, and disease;

Absence of attachment, refusal to be wrapped up in one's children, wife, home and family, even-mindedness whether good or ill befall;

Unwavering and all-exclusive devotion to me, resort to secluded spots, distaste for the haunts of men;

Settled conviction of the nature of the *Aatman*, a perception of the goal of the knowledge of Truth;

All this is declared to be Knowledge and the reverse of it is ignorance.

- Bhagavad Gita

POVERTY is bold and ruthless. Poverty needs no plans/schedules.

RICHES is shy and timid. RICHES needs to be attracted. RICHES requires schedules. In any way, a person never loses anything. Instead, he/she indeed becomes RICH and has riches in proportion to how he/ she applies these schedules.

The Receiving Schedule is to make YOU ready for receiving the RESULTS in the SS, as well as to know YOU. The RS is just like a FOG; while the knowledge in the RS clears the fog, and when it clears, you are in the Supreme Schedule, which results in Abundance.

You don't need a degree to get knowledge in the RS, but just read to accept the Receiving Schedule.

ACCEPTANCE is the SECRET.

Most successful people and the richest people gained riches after 40+ age, i.e., in the SS. Most billionaires in the world are 40+, i.e., they are in their SS. You don't always need money to make money, even if you start from scratch, as long as you start at the right time, i.e., in the RS. Most of us think that it is tough to be RICH or make MONEY.

Yes, it is hard, but not very hard, and most us already do tough work in life, even without keeping MONEY in the

HC: Aim–Money–Purpose, and hard work is already done in the PS. Moreover, the tough part will be done for us in the Supreme Schedule by FREE.

You are in the RS (30-40 years of age) now. Never think of leaving the HC. Just be with your HC, even if you have not done well with your HC, either Aim or Money. If you want, just choose another Aim, make an HC, and go ahead. Just be in the RS, withholding your HC through HC Plans and Goals/Targets. Most importantly, you will know that YOU become FREE in the Receiving Schedule. In the Supreme Schedule, the RESULTS part, you make no effort at all in real. Your role is not to think about the RESULTS, but just to know/follow the Receiving Schedule.

If you want to think about RESULTS, then think what is that which works for RESULTS.inside us that will work for the RESULTS part for us? That is FREE.

You will know about the Receiving Schedule now. The hardest part of the HC is the RESULTS that FREE plays for us. You will know FREE in the Receiving Schedule.

By action alone, before you reach the Supreme Schedule for RESULTS for your HC, you should know FREE.

Action alone is your province, not the RESULTS. FREE plays the RESULTS part for your HC.

Your role is to prepare for your HC in the PS and know FREE in the RS. By birth, you were FREE from all, but when your senses come into contact with objects, you have desires which overtake your FREE. You can again be FREE from all as well as you get your HC.

The exciting thing is that your HC comes to us ITSELF when YOU become FREE from all. The solution is knowing FREE and following Gratitude and Surrender.

Your HC as well as money, health, happiness, harmonious relationships and a harmonious life come to us themselves and that too in ABUNDANCE when your SELF becomes FREE from all.

FREE never means to leave something (your thoughts, desires, ideas, plans, goals, beliefs, knowledge), but to go beyond them by becoming one with them (your thoughts, ideas, plans, goals, beliefs, knowledge) by becoming FREE.

By GRATITUDE and SURRENDER, FREE can be KNOWN and truely entered into FREE .

So, you will know FREE in the Receiving Schedule. You were born FREE, one with the billions and the SUPREME and full of Gratitude.

The RS is mainly the RECEIVING of the KNOWLEDGE. It is the FREE level 2 and the setting of plans, goals/targets of the HC is the Harmonious Combination level 2.

Those who did not follow the PS consciously can also start with the Receiving Schedule because they too have followed some PS consciously or unconsciously. But they should read the PS to get the ideas clear, so that they may understand the RS well.

In the RS, for FREE level 2, you know, knowledge of YOU / FREE.

For HC level 2, YOU will have Plans, goals and setting of plans, long and short, regarding your HC and the extended plans till the last (80+) of your HC .

We were born FREE from all. In the SS (0–14 years of age), you are born Free, but as soon as your senses come in contact with objects, you have desires, and thus you make an HC, and you write down your HC in the PS.

After writing your HC, there are 2 things -

1.Make ready your HC

4.Ready to receive your HC

Make ready your HC means to prepare your HC, which you have done in the PS, i.e., faith, HC thoughts chanting, constant practice, visualization, and timetable. But, you get ready to RECEIVE the RESULTS (RESULTS of HC and HC related things: H, H, HR, HL in abundance) in the RS. It is very EASY, you just need to be FREE. FREE is very easy; you just need to KNOW it.

Why be FREE?

Because you were born FREE and you are searching for it too. Your HC and HC related things, i.e., H, H, HR, HL, come to you by themselves in REALITY and ABUNDANCE, when YOU/SELF becomes FREE from all .

Let's start.

If you did not follow the PS, then you may have non-HC thoughts, beliefs, habits, and ideas about Aim, Money, and Purpose, i.e., about your HC. Let's precise habits, beliefs, and ideas first.

What thoughts, ideas, beliefs, and habits are you following? Know it, Write it. In the PS, you have HC thoughts. You have HC ideas, habits, beliefs.

In the Receiving Schedule, you know what beliefs you are following. Know your beliefs, ideas, and habits.

They lead us towards your plans and goals of the HC; HC beliefs, HC ideas, HC plans, HC behavior about your HC, i.e., about aim, money, and purpose.

Your HC beliefs, HC ideas, HC plans, HC behavior etc. will overcome the bondage (bondage is an unnecessary worry, fear, doubt, question) about your HC–health, happiness, harmonious relationships, a harmonious life. Writing is essential. This book has given you the space on the left side to write and check where you are.

By writing on the side page, we track the HC beliefs, habits, ideas, plans, and goals in the RS. The Receiving Schedule is very important. Usually, you know the PS and the SS. You typically go from the PS to the Supreme Schedule without knowing. Knowledge is in the RS. PS has preparation, while the SS has surrender and RESULTS.

Receiving Schedule gives knowledge by reading only. You don't need a degree to understand the RS or recite something, but just to identify some concepts of YOU, the billions, etc. by reading .Then the Supreme Schedule becomes wonderful and complete.

In the RS, those who have not followed the HC thoughts or may have followed the non-HC thoughts consciously or unconsciously, they may have limited beliefs and habits about the HC and the riches and wealth in the SC Mind. You need to replace those limited beliefs and habits with HC habits, beliefs, ideas.

Habits, Beliefs, Ideas -

In the Receiving Schedule, your HC thoughts/HC beliefs/HC habits originate from the storage of your SC Mind, which you stored in the PS by following the PS, HC thoughts. These HC thoughts/HC beliefs/HC habits are mixed with the HC ideas and plans, thus becoming CREATIVE. What you follow/hear/experience/see when you are young in the PS, becomes your HC thoughts/HC beliefs/HC habits.

The Preparing Schedule is to nurture and nourish your SC Mind so that the SC Mind has great beliefs, feelings of the HC and great habits in the RS. Because the non-HC beliefs and habits settle in the SC Mind, they are a little complicated to change, but can still be changed. Those who have followed the PS have HC habits, beliefs, and ideas. Now, the SC mind accepts only the HC habits, beliefs, and ideas.

You should check your beliefs about MONEY, WEALTH and YOURSELF. The HC beliefs, habits, thoughts and feelings, which you gained in the PS, have become your TRUTH. These truths are the tools for gaining knowledge in the Receiving Schedule.

Know what your beliefs are about MONEY, AIM and PURPOSE (i.e., HC); what your habits are regarding MONEY, AIM, and PURPOSE (i.e., HC); what your feelings and beliefs are about YOURSELF. These habits and beliefs are your truth and you usually seek their refuge whenever you face any new challenge or success in your Aim, Money, and Purpose (i.e., HC). You use, experiment, try these truths of your beliefs and check how valid these beliefs are in daily life whenever you go for new challenges regarding your Aim, Money, and Purpose (i.e., HC), then your HC beliefs, habits, ideas counter them.

The more they counter/cherish the challenge/success, the more your HC. beliefs, habits, ideas become stronger.

Habits -

"You are what you repeatedly do. Excellence then is not an act, but a habit."

-Aristotle

A habit is a routine behavior that is regularly repeated. A habit is a fixed way of thinking or feeling, gained through the previous repetition of a mental experience. Habit formation is the process by which a behavior, through regular repetition, becomes automatic.

The thoughts/actions which you repeat again and again become a habit. We are creatures of habit; we build our lives on patterns of thoughts, beliefs, ideas, emotions and behavior. You should have HC habits, so these trends which grow lead to easiness. You should set a most significant HC to challenge yourself, thus increase your mental, emotional and physical strength.

Most of your habits are formed in the PS, i.e., during a young age. Your PS is so high that it creates the best HC behavior and HC habits in us. If you have followed the PS consciously, then you have HC habits, beliefs, ideas about HC.

If you have non-HC habits, then you need to change your non-HC habits into HC habits because the non-HC habits are obstacles which get created in your HC and in knowing FREE.

You can change your non-HC habits in the RS by following the RS consciously. Have the HC habit of saving money and use the money for investment, daily expenses, etc.

Have the HC habit to think towards your purpose. The richest persons in the world follow these HC habits–they keep learning, they read good books, they are economical with money, they learn from their mistakes, they focus on what they like. You should make the habit of managing even a small amount of money. It may be $1or $100.

It is more important than the amount because later when you are RICH, you should have the same habit of managing a significant amount of money. Habits matter.

If you have the habit of managing Money, then whether it is small or large, the habit will handle it. Learn the habit to be spiritual with money and manage it even when your income is not very much, because only the HC habits lead you closer to your HC. The rewards of HC habits are that you will go through the RS very easily. So important are the HC habits, they make the RS easy.

You prepared your HC in the PS and made HC habits there; that's the excellent part of the PS.

Beliefs -

Belief is trust; that which you think is true without any proof, for those who followed the PS have HC beliefs. Others who don't have HC beliefs should change them in the RS. For example: the non-HC belief that becoming RICH or making MONEY is very difficult; you need to replace them with HC beliefs. You should do it in the RS.

If we think our ideas, beliefs, and habits are non-HC, we may replace them in the RS. Replace the limited beliefs with HC beliefs regarding the abundance and excess of money; that there is a flow of money which comes from multiple sources; I am getting RICH steadily; money comes easily to me, I have a spiritual relationship with money.

Have these HC beliefs about Aim, Money, and Purpose in the RS.

SC mind bondage (questions, worry, doubt, fear) in the Preparing Schedule checks your FAITH; in the RS, it tests your beliefs. So, have the HC beliefs to overcome bondage and move up from HC 2 and Free Level 2.

Ideas -

Ideas are formed by gathering information related to your HC. You need HC thoughts for HC, which you followed in the PS. These HC thoughts and the values and principles you developed in the PS come together in a cluster to become an IDEA, and you become ready to follow a great IDEA. You may have ideas from the old combinations of thoughts and mix them up with new views. All the HC thoughts you developed in the PS are ready to form an IDEA, or going towards following a great IDEA.

As you have the choice to place HC thoughts in the Finite mind, similarly you have the choice to place great ideas in the SC mind.

An IDEA will take us in the RS to the SS (i.e., from Free level 2 / HC desire level 2 to Free level 3 / HC level 3). If you don't place an IDEA in the SC Mind, the place would remain vacant resulting in an unused SC Mind.

Write down 5-8 ideas for the SC Mind -

1. Action alone is a great Harmonious Combination idea; Ideas have strong emotions and will impress the best of the SC Mind in the Restoring Schedule.

2. FREE plays the RESULTS part for your HC

3. You need not think about the RESULTS in the PS or the RS. In the SS, you need not think about the RESULTS at all.

4. Your HC not only has Aim, Money, and Purpose, but also health, happiness, harmonious relationships and a harmonious life.

5. Riches is a state of mind.

6. M, h, h, hr, hl, will come to you themselves like the many great ideas.

Action alone is thy province, not the RESULTS. This is one of the best ideas in the Gita.

Money, health, happiness, harmonious relationships and a harmonious life come to us themselves when YOU/SELF become FREE. FREE is an IDEA too. The RS is also related to IDEAS. In the RS, you should know these IDEAS and express them and give them the term 'FREE'. You should present to your subconscious mind an HC plan, a great HC thought, IDEA and PURPOSE related to your HC. So, you have filled the space which is meant for a plan, a great HC thought, IDEA and PURPOSE pertaining to your HC in the subconscious mind. In addition, you will notice that your SC Mind automatically engages you in your plan, IDEA and PURPOSE related to your HC in the RS.

Behavior -

Your beliefs, habits, and ideas make your behavior and build your behavioral pattern towards your HC and HC related things. The more you have HC habits, beliefs and ideas, the more you develop the HC behavior and behavioral pattern.

Plans -

You are now ready to follow the RS 30+ and may start straight from the RS.

Try to understand the following brief overview of the receiving schedules of the HC.

Set your HC plan now. Set your current year's HC plan and the following year's HC plan.

Divide your yearly HC plan into months and days and start following it every day.

HC plan for the current year:

1.What do you want to do this year?

2. How much money do you want to have this year?

3. What is your social motive for this year?

4. Your other wishes?

By writing your HC plans, goals/targets, you confirm that you are with your HC and you want to complete to the RS for your HC now, so that you go to the SS then for the RESULTS of your HC. Also, make a plan for HC in the RS for 5 years or 10 years, because the Receiving Schedule is for 10 years, then divide them into quarterly goals/targets. Along with that, set 20/40 years' plans for the time until the last. Those who did not follow the PS and have not set an HC, and are now in the Receiving Schedule (30-40 age group)may start from here because if they have followed the Preparing Schedule even unconsciously, it is good. However, they would have to read the PS well, to grasp the PS, so that they will be able to follow the RS well. They should set their HC plan; if they have already prepared their HC, it is good; if they have not, they should find out what they like to do the most. It may be even be just a hobby. Find it out, make an HC and then plan for it. Planning involves the action steps required to achieve some specific goal.

Therefore, you reduce the necessary time and effort required to achieve a goal. Plan what you are going to do with your HC level 2 of the HC in the RS, i.e., in 10 years. Set the HC plan for 5 years, then 10 years and divide it yearly, i.e., moving from the skills of the aim to plan how to create VALUE for your PRODUCT.

What is your PRODUCT?

Usually, your AIM is the PRODUCT, but in real, YOU are the PRODUCT; the great FAITH, values and principles made us a PRODUCT with great VALUE. The skills you learned in the PS for your AIM made your PRODUCT, now you need to plan how to make a value of it in the market, so you need to know/create/increase the value of your product. You need to create the VALUE of your PRODUCT in terms of money and plan about MONEY (cash + net worth) and your PURPOSE. You don't need to be a specialist in the market for creating a market VALUE of your product and knowledge of money.

You are lucky that you live in the internet age. You can have a lot of information online and use it without any cost. Just be persistent and slowly, you will find the way.

First, you should create the VALUE of your PRODUCT. MONEY defines the VALUE of your PRODUCT/SKILL/RICHES/WEALTH, which is the overall VALUE of your PRODUCT and KNOWLEDGE of YOU. You need to PLAN on how to create a value for your PRODUCT. Just know that the more you grow with your FREE level 2 and HC level 2, the higher will be the VALUE of your PRODUCT. You have the RS for it. Increase the value of the product in the RS. You will have creative thoughts and IDEAS in the RS by knowing the SC Mind and YOU/FREE.

Let's come again to the RS plan. Divide your yearly HC plan into months. Make a plan of action for everyday and ACT on it EVERYDAY.

So, to plan for your FREE level 2 in the RS is to go beyond the SC Mind to YOU, then to the billions and the SUPREME in the RS. This is the FREE level 2 plan for 10 years in the RS. Just make a rough extended PLAN for your HC till the last of the SS (till 80+), i.e., a 40 years' PLAN because you want your HC till the last, as well as you wish H, H, HR, HL till the end of the SS. In the RS, i.e., in the 10 years, you will create a value of your PRODUCT; this is HC LEVEL 2. In addition, in the Supreme Schedule, you will get the PRICE (cash–the amount you have set for the product–... million US $) and set a plan of a net worth of amount... Billion US $, until the last of the SS for your product, and similarly to establish a plan for your PURPOSE until the end of the SS. You should make one or more detailed plans to achieve your goals with the available resources. Identify the goals to be completed, create strategies to achieve them with the available resources of your time, money, and other resources for attaining your goals. Put them to use and monitor all the steps in their proper order. You may take some calculated risks to increase the value of your PRODUCT. The goal of your PLANS in the RS should be to move towards creating a VALUE of your PRODUCT.

You will be paid in proportion to the value of your PRODUCT in the marketplace. Another way of understanding it is to INCREASE the VALUE of your PRODUCT to answer the following questions: How many people do you serve by your product? The more people you serve, the higher the value of your product. Don't hurry. You have 10 years in the RS (30-40 years).

Again, remember, ACTION alone...

Well-chosen goals in the PLAN keep us in the right direction and keep us on the right track. It tells you where you want to go and exactly how to get there. It increases your effectiveness and makes you more efficient.

Write down your goals to achieve within the year and so on. In the RS plan, goals should cover your day-to-day work, solutions which check the challenges that you encounter in your PLAN, acquisition of new skills and creativeness.

Keep each goal clear and simple. Be specific. Be realistic.

Don't hurry, make sure that your goals are in harmony with your purpose (Ultimate Aim). Meanwhile, you may have some part-time/full-time work to have a smooth life. It will not change your PLAN at all.

If you have the resources, you may start a small startup. You may start with joining a group of people related to your business or aim. You share your IDEAS and PLANS and work out a plan. Your own business is the best way to become wealthy. If you don't have the resources, you may have a job.

I was a waiter between 30-40 years age, i.e., in the RS, but my book PLAN was going along with my job still. If you have a job then you are at least living comfortably, and IDEAS come when you are comfortable. Making a short or long-term plan and setting the goals/targets for it should be a habit in the RS. Write your plans and goals precisely in every detail.

Write it down. Write them, read whenever you get a chance. Make a list that will lead you towards your goal.

Constantly act on the to-do list. Your HC plan has some HC goals.

Write down your HC goal heads-

ACT effortlessly on these HC goal heads every day.

1. HC goal head

2. HC goal head

3. Money head

4. Purpose head

5. Other heads

Write the heads of HC related to your HC goals. You may write some HC goal heads pertaining to your HC, such as health, happiness, harmonious relationships and a harmonious life.

Write/read these statements-

1. I am with my HC goals.

2. I have prepared my HC in the PS.

3. I am with my RS of the HC.

4. I am conscious of my HC desire for MONEY and other HC goals.

5. I understand the HC, HC plans, goals, targets.

6. I understand the Finite mind and the SC Mind.

7. I am moving towards the SS, i.e., from Free level2/ HC level 2 to Free level 3/HC level 3.

8. I am following the POG (The PRACTICE of GRATITUDE).

By following the HC PLAN/goals of your HC in the RS, you are moving towards the SS.

Constantly apply the HC ideas, HC thoughts in the HC PLAN, i.e., of aim, money and ultimate aim (Purpose). Do not hurry, but act constantly and harmoniously.

Money

Money is the value of your product which you prepared in the PS.

Wealth = (Cash/MONEY + net valuable things)

WEALTH is the overall value of your product and the knowledge of YOU/FREE which you will know in the RS. Wealth has a significant value of assets, including cash-money, along with a good number of available hours. Those who are looking to start up, don't think that you need a lot of money to start a business, or need loans and so many permits, etc. Sometimes, it does not require money to make money.

You become financially sound when money comes from the INCOME as well as other sources, i.e., bonds, shares, property, and gold value. You become financially sound when your INCOME exceeds your expenses.

Money affects your life in a big way. If you manage your money well in the RS, with savings, investments and expenses, your overall life will become harmonious. Later in the Supreme Schedule, when you have more money, you may have a financial adviser and manager. They will manage your money and money accounts. There will be many options to invest then. In the RS, most of us are doing our jobs or managing our startups along with keeping our HC in our mind. So, you have the income from your job/business. You should follow simple living and high thinking. That is, be economical while spending. Thus, you have more savings, which means more room for investment.

There are many live examples of rich people who can become your role models. They are living such simple lives while very focused on savings for investments and keeping their expenses less. Live a simple life with high values, following Brahmacharya, the highest way of simple living. In the Receiving Schedule, learn the habit of saving, investment and minimize your expenses. With some part of your savings, you may join some professional classes on money regarding investments or something related to your PRODUCT. Usually, as your income rises, your expenses also rise; here your habit of saving will come into use. Those who have the Aim to have a business may start a startup from scratch in the RS. The best way to be RICH is by having your own business or PRODUCT. Keep in mind the amount you wrote in Money and net worth in your HC. The value of your PRODUCT will reach very close to that amount, and the NET worth will be the overall value of the PRODUCT and the Knowledge which you receive in the Receiving Schedule. You have already worked hard to prepare your PRODUCT in the PS, now you just need to create/increase its value. You are lucky that you are in the internet world. You can gain any knowledge regarding your PRODUCT, its PLANS and about savings and investments.

It can all be known online. You can get the basic knowledge to start up anytime. Have a spiritual relationship with business; money makes us happier, secure and harmonious, and helps us purchase good books, and in traveling, etc. Money is wonderful and gives us many choices to use it in a better way. When you have more money, it will provide you the extra time to spend on your business/PRODUCT. The average millionaire lives a modest life.80% of them are 40+ in age or older. Most of them became RICH in the Supreme Schedule. They like reading great books, are self-made, have good habits, like sports, exercising for good health, have good eating habits, like to help others succeed in life, are charitable and have financial advisers. They have a simple living with their families and spouses, plan their day every day, wake up early everyday, are economical, have been to college and universities, and take calculated risks.

They work a lot and enjoy with a good friend circle and family, have a company of good and successful people, appreciate talent, riches and other successful people. They help others to be rich and successful, are good citizens and obey rules, have a good team of people, have multiple sources of income and are honest. They also invest in government bonds; the government takes many initiatives to make people aware of the investment bonds. Thus, people benefit from secure government bonds and the government gets money for developmental purposes. They find out who the best investors are, find out what they're buying and buy what they buy to follow them. They are smart and rich. They put up huge returns every year regardless of what the market does. Just one of these stocks could let you retire rich. Most importantly, this investing lets you enjoy your life. These investors bet on sure things. They invest in things they know very well, so only buy the stocks that the world's best billionaire investors own discount. Hold these stocks, enjoy life and wait until the returns are good, then sell them when the billionaire investors sell, and repeat.

The Sub-Conscious Mind -

There is a hierarchy,

1.Finite mind

2.Supreme Consciousness mind

3.YOU / FREE

4.The billions

5.The SUPREME

6.The POG (the Practice of Gratitude), the POS (the Practice of Surrender)

We have known the Finite Mind and the SC Mind in the PS,

We will study the rest of them now.

Sub-Consciousness MIND

The SC mind has 7-8 things to know -

It stores thoughts and feelings you enjoyed, repeated (chanted) and the ones held by the conscious mind in the PS (14–30 years of age)

It is the house of your habits and beliefs. The thoughts and feelings you enjoyed, repeated, chanted and held in the conscious mind in the Preparing Schedule (14–30 years of age) forms beliefs based on those thoughts and feelings in the SC mind. You will have those ideas and habits during the RS (30–40 years of age).

3. The SC mind likes the feel-good factors. The subconscious does not see any difference between HC thoughts and non-HC thoughts. The thoughts which you repeat (by chanting), hold the longest, enjoy whether consciously or unconsciously, the subconscious mind takes as true and stores it by taking it from the conscious mind. The SC mind stores those thoughts which make the SC mind feel good, because the SC mind doesn't know true or false, it only knows what makes it feel good. E.g., even if you are not rich, if you feel rich, the SC mind will get an impression of being rich and you will succeed in telling

the SC mind that you want to be rich and have riches. Your SC mind will then have a great feeling, belief and habit of being RICH.

4. It has bondage, questions, worry, fear, doubts, thus creates unnecessary problems.

Points 1, 2, 3 and 4 you have known in the Preparing Schedule (14–30 years of age). Points 5, 6, 7, and 8 you will know in the Receiving Schedule (30–40 years of age) now.

5. It is the NO THOUGHT PART of the mind. It does not think like the Finite mind, so it does not have thoughts like the F mind. So, it is the NO thought part of the mind.

6. The SC Mind like to follow the deepest HC thoughts, HC plans and HC IDEAS.

7. The SC mind likes effortlessness, and it works automatically, e.g., it controls your breath, the mind and the heartbeat. You know you don't make any conscious effort in breathing and in beating the heart. Just so, the SC mind works automatically on HC plans and HC ideas, if the HC plans and HC ideas are presented to the SC mind. It likes effortlessness.

8. The SC Mind also has a connection with the SUPREME, so it likes, knows and helps in your Purpose too.

You are in the RS by your past thinking in the PS, by your thought processes which you followed, whether consciously or unconsciously. Many of us have had HC thoughts unconsciously.

As you studied in the Preparing Schedule, the SC mind stores the HC thoughts of your HC, which you keep/

chant in your Finite mind, e.g., you had the HC thoughts & experienced that becoming rich is EASY. You have kept it in your mind, you have a great purpose and aim to be rich, and you followed the rich's experiences, so your SC mind took it as TRUE.

In the Receiving Schedule, the sub-conscious mind is stronger than the finite mind, so these chanted, held, enjoyed Harmonious Combination

become your behavior, habit patterns and knowledge in the Receiving Schedule. The Finite mind was the teacher of the SC mind (student) in the PS. If the teacher teaches HC thoughts and feelings to the student (SC mind), then the student will have good experiences in the Receiving Schedule because of the HC thoughts and feelings that it was taught.

These HC thoughts and feelings which the finite mind repeated, chanted, held and enjoyed, will become the Knowledge of the SC mind in the Receiving Schedule. The SC mind will display these thoughts and feelings in the RS. It will also be helpful to know FREE. The SC mind is hereditary too, while also getting ideas, thoughts, and experiences from home, business and social surroundings and others' opinions, suggestions or statements as well.

But if you have chanted, repeated and held your HC thoughts and feelings consciously, then these HC thoughts and feelings will be the DOMINATING thoughts. Thus, you deliberately influenced your SC mind for your HC because you need the SC mind in the Receiving Schedule (30–40 years of age; Free level 2 / HC desire level 2). That's why you have focused only on the HC thoughts in the Preparing Schedule, so that the subconscious mind is ready in the Receiving Schedule (Free level 2 / desire level 2) to know FREE. Finally, it would take us to the SS (Free level 3 / HC desire level 3).

Wherever the fickle and unsteady mind wanders, thence should it be reined, and brought under the sole sway of the Aatman.

- Bhagavad Gita

You had the HC thoughts in the PS so that your RS would become very easy, since the subconscious mind likes things easy and effortless. If you have followed the HC thoughts chanting in the PS, then only can your SC mind be easy in the Receiving Schedule. It need not work in the RS, it will be very easy, thus YOU will be very easy in the RS because out of the total, the conscious mind is just 10%, while the SC mind occupies 90% of the mind. In the Preparing Schedule, you are using just 5-6% of the conscious mind if you are following the HC thoughts chanting. In the RS, you need not depend on chanting the HC thoughts in the Finite mind, but follow the practice of Gratitude and HSOM (Harmonious State of Mind) which is a kind of meditation Practice for the SC Mind and takes only 15-20 minutes of your time every day! It'll help to know YOU/FREE.

In the PS, the finite mind is very active (before the 30s), but after that the SC mind becomes active. The SC mind likes IDEAS, PLANS, and some very best of HC thoughts, while also wanting to know YOU/FREE. You learn to use the consciousness (no-thought part) of the SC mind for your HC in the RS through the harmonious state of Mind (HSOM, a kind of meditation exercise). It will take you closer to know YOU/FREE. You have known the HC thoughts chanting in the PS, and now you shall know the consciousness of the SC mind through the HSOM exercise in the RS. After following the HSOM in the Receiving Schedule, you know FREE, and you become FREE. FREE plays the RESULTS part for your HC.

Now, you have selected the HC thoughts/HC ideas to keep in mind in the RS because you start to use the consciousness (no-thought part) of the SC mind more and more as compared to the finite mind (HC thoughts chanting) when in the RS. The SC mind has consciousness (no thinking part). By knowing the no thinking part of the SC mind, we go beyond the Finite mind to the SC mind, and then to YOU/FREE. In the RS, bondage of the SC mind is there, but only a little. That bondage of the SC mind is to stop us from doing the non-HC things or to warn us about them.

The above is applicable in the Preparing Schedule, Receiving Schedule and the Supreme Schedule as well. Whenever we do non-HC things, the bondage of the SC mind warns us. This is the beauty of the SC mind; it reminds us not to do the non-HC things. But, if this is happening in the case of HC things as well, we certainly should overcome the bondage. Regarding the bondage of the SC Mind for HC, it checks the strength of your beliefs.

The SC mind is connected with the SUPREME. You cannot follow your subconscious mind like your Finite Mind, but you can make your SC mind harmonious every day by HSOM exercise, i.e., you can keep your SC mind more and more harmonious every day. The SC mind does not think like the Finite mind. Simply know your SC mind as a no-thought part of the mind. The SC Mind does not think; it works without thinking for your HC. The HSOM exercise (a kind of meditation but with open eyes) can make us aware of the no-thought part and enable us to enter into the sub-consciousness and connect with the SUPREME at a deeper and most profound level. It allows us to experience the awareness of the SC mind which is not possible through thoughts, i.e., through the Finite mind. The Finite mind knows something through thoughts, but to know the consciousness (no thought part) of the SC mind is not possible through thoughts. It is possible through no thoughts however, i.e., through the HSOM exercise.

As you start the RS, you should go from the finite mind to the SC mind, i.e., from HC thoughts chanting to the no thoughts or consciousness (no thought part of the SC mind) by HSOM exercise. You may follow the HSOM exercise for 15-20 minutes in the morning and the evening.

You have known the Finite Mind through the HC thoughts chanting in the PS; you will now know the SC Mind through HSOM exercise.

Take a room where you can be alone and undisturbed. Follow this practice by sitting in a relaxed posture on a chair. Sit erect and comfortably, but do not lie ;just relax, tongue curled up, mouth a little open, chin a little up, eyes blinking smoothly, and slow down. Be very easy, doing and thinking nothing of the body or the mind, just sit, knowing the consciousness (no thoughts part) of the SC mind for your HC.

You may draw a circle on the wall, and look straight at it, just to make sure that you are not doing anything but the HSOM exercise which allow us to relax 100%. Focus now on your breathing; breathe in by your nose and breathe out by your mouth smoothly, take deep breaths in start, then let it be smooth, automatic, and effortless. Slow and comfortable with each breath, be more and more relaxed and easy. As your body rests, the mind will go deep into the no-thought part. This is a very harmonious experience.

When you start doing HSOM, the HC thoughts start becoming one with the no thought part (the SC mind, no thinking part) and the HSOM start growing gradually. You have 15–20 minutes to follow the HSOM exercise. In the beginning of the first 5 minutes of the HSOM exercise, you may chant the main/best HC thoughts, and in the next 5 minutes, you may place your plans and ideas of your HC in the SC Mind. Finally, in the last 10 minutes, no HC thoughts chanting, and no placing the ideas and plans. Then slowly going towards the no thinking part only, focus on the circle and breathe. Know that the HSOM exercise is to move from the F mind to the SC Mind (no thought part). This 15 to 20 minutes of HSOM exercise when done every morning and evening daily, will drive you to know the consciousness (the no thought part) of the SC Mind during the day for your HC.

HSOM exercise makes you choose the best HC thoughts of your HC, so the HC thoughts become more focused and powerful in the HSOM exercise. HSOM exercise means the time to relax the finite mind and use the SC mind more. In the Receiving Schedule, you don't use the finite mind as much as you use it in the Preparing Schedule. You use the finite mind but for chanting very selected HC thoughts in the RS.

You use the HSOM exercise in the RS as your subconscious loves to do the work for your HC plans. So, you should follow the HSOM exercise, since you have worked for your HC by the finite mind through HC thoughts chanting in the Preparing Schedule, and now in the RS, you would work for your HC plans by using the consciousness (no thought part) of the SC mind. By HSOM, you gain the knowledge of the SC mind (no thinking part–it's the essence of FREE) and you become firm in your HC plans and comes closer to FREE.

By HSOM exercise, you choose the best HC thoughts, place your ideas and plans in the SC Mind, and the sub-conscious mind starts working for your HC through the plans and ideas which you put during the HSOM exercise. By HSOM exercise, you keep your SC Mind in USE during the whole day because you are doing the HSOM exercise. Thus, you are keeping your SC Mind open during the whole day for your HC to get creative HC thoughts and ideas, plans, etc. In the PS, you do HC thoughts chanting during the day in your Finite mind, but in the Receiving Schedule, you follow the HSOM exercise two times, morning and evening daily, and you chant the HC thoughts, and place your ideas and plans in SC Mind during the HSOM exercise. It allows you to keep your SC Mind open for the rest of the day. If you have any HC thoughts, ideas or plans coming to your Mind and you find it creative, just write it down and put it in the HSOM exercise the next day.

So, your whole day has an open SC Mind, getting the best HC thoughts, HC plans, and ideas. That's the main reason you are following the HSOM exercise. This is the way of using the SC Mind (no thinking part) in the Receiving Schedule. This is a way you can have an open SC Mind during the whole day to have the best HC thoughts, HC plans, and ideas by following the HSOM exercise. And you will have a Harmonious State of Mind (HSOM) for the whole day too. The subconscious mind is the connecting link between the finite mind and the SUPREME.

The sub-conscious mind likes your purpose, and the Supreme loves your purpose. The sub-conscious mind is thus connected with the SUPREME through your PURPOSE of the HC. As the SUPREME is infinite, so the SC mind being a part of the Supreme is also infinite. HC thoughts chanting is the meditation of the finite mind. It's the highest level of consciousness of the finite mind.

Similarly, the HSOM exercise is the highest level of consciousness (no thoughts part) of the SC mind. Your FREE level 2 / HC level 2 grows as you depend upon the sub-conscious mind in the RS. You become very EASY. The more you are dependent upon the subconscious in the Receiving Schedule, the more harmonious your HC thoughts, plans, ideas will become. That is how the PS (for the Finite Mind) and RS (for the SC Mind and YOU) are made. The subconscious will carry out the plans and ideas which you placed in the HSOM exercise; non-bondage, the best HC thoughts and feelings, HC ideas and plans, brahmacharya, all these grow in the SC Mind.

By the HSOM exercise, you use your SC mind for your HC plans as well as make your SC mind harmonious. The knowledge in the RS and HSOM exercise will change the limited belief in ABUNDANCE. HSOM has focused attention for your HC plans/goals. HSOM will lead towards health, happiness, harmonious relationships, and a harmonious life to abundance and riches. Usually, you are with a state of mind in the RS; it may be an HC state of mind or a non-HC state of mind. But if you follow the HSOM, you certainly are with the HSOM and your HC plans/goals and grow your FREE level 2/HC level 2. By HSOM, your HC habits and HC beliefs become the TRUTH, and they are helpful in your HC plans/goals to know YOU/FREE.

These HC beliefs and HC habits about your HC as 'the Truth' become the HSOM as well. Usually, those who are not with the HSOM don't know that they are not with the HSOM because it's their beliefs and habits that are moving them.

They are reacting according to their beliefs and habits. But those who are following the HSOM exercise are consciously moving by the HC beliefs and HC habits for their HC plans/goals.

Those who did not follow the PS consciously, may follow the HSOM exercise now. It will change their practices and beliefs into HC habits and beliefs. That's what HSOM is designed to do, so that all the energy goes towards your HC plans/goals.

HC plans/goals become easy, natural and effortless. No willpower, no HC chanting is needed now, as you can do this through the HSOM.

It is a simple but powerful tool that energizes your SC Mind. HSOM exercise is natural. It is focusing your attention towards your HC plans, knowing the no thought part of the SC mind, or a focused consciousness of the no thought part of the SC mind for your HC plans.

You naturally want to go to the HSOM in the RS after following the PS, and will be with the HSOM throughout the day.

The main purpose of using the HSOM exercise is to know your SC Mind and to have a Harmonious State of Mind for the whole day. The HSOM exercise talks directly to your SC Mind. HSOM overcomes all the remaining bondage of the SC mind. HSOM involves a 'no-thought' process. It is a way to move towards YOU/FREE. In the HSOM exercise, you go to the SC Mind to make it harmonious for your HC plans/goals because by following the HSOM exercise, the more your SC mind becomes harmonious, the more comfortable your HC plans/goals will become.

When a man puts away all the cravings that arise in his mind and finds comfort for himself only from the Atman, he is then called a man of firm understanding.

- Bhagavad Gita

And you will get closer to know YOU/FREE. The Finite mind prepares your PS by having HC thoughts, and the SC mind prepares creativity in your HC by the HSOM exercise. Placing HC ideas, plans/goals in it.

Action alone is the highest IDEA for the SC mind; it would take you to the SS. Only 10% is the finite mind, out of which you use 5-6% if you are following the HC thoughts to chant. 90% is the SC mind, out of which more than 50% is consciousness (no thought part) and the rest, less than 40%, is for ideas, plans, HC thoughts, ultimate aim/purpose, feelings, emotions, imagination, beliefs and habits (what you repeat in the Preparing Schedule by the conscious mind, the SC mind will repeat in the RS).

Whenever you feel like you are overthinking to stressed, follow the HSOM exercise. HSOM exercise is to know the difference between the finite mind and the SC mind. HSOM is to the SC mind what thinking is to the finite mind. SC mind has no thoughts, it is beyond thoughts; the SC mind knows YOU.

The SC mind understands only one language now, THE BILLIONS. The SC mind only listens to the voice of all the billions. Connect your SC mind with the billions.

You can connect your SC mind with the billions by giving gratitude to the Supreme from all of us billions, and by giving appreciation to the billions in the practice of Gratitude everyday.

The SC mind listens to the billions, connects with the billions in your POG and will overcome all the bondage (questions/worry/fear/doubt) and make us know YOU very clearly. The SC Mind likes IDEAS.

Present to your subconscious mind (the SC Mind) the IDEA–Money, health, happiness, harmonious relationships and a harmonious life. They will come to YOU by themselves when your SELF becomes FREE from all.

You are now carefully selecting only the limited HC IDEAS for your HC.

HC ideas and action alone...M, H, h, hr, hl, W comes to us.

With the harmonious feelings of gratitude for the billions in your SC mind, you and the billions are connected. With the harmonious feelings of gratitude in your SC mind, you start enjoying everything, i.e., health, happiness, a harmonious life and harmonious relationships.

This is a precondition to begin receiving your HC; you start enjoying health, happiness, harmonious relations and a harmonious life. It means that you are prepared entirely by your minds to receive your HC.

With the feeling of gratitude in your SC mind, your SC mind accepts the arrangements that are being made for your HC, for us billions and between the billions, and the bondage (q/w/f/d) of the SC mind is overcome.

Present your HC plan to your subconscious mind now.

Experience yourself the working of the SC mind through the HC plan for your desire for MONEY(set the HC goal on a quarterly basis in your HC plan)every day.

Therefore with the sword of self-realization, sever thou this doubt, bred of ignorance, which has crept into thy heart! Betake thyself to yoga and arise!

- Bhagavad Gita

You have moved from the finite mind in the PS to the SC mind in the RS, and then beyond the SC mind comes YOU, i.e., FREE.

You have known the F mind and the SC mind, and now you will realize YOU, the billions, the SUPREME and the POG (Practice of Gratitude).

YOU / FREE

Know that to be imperishable whereby all this is pervaded, no one can destroy that immutable being.

- Bhagavad Gita

As there is thought (in the Finite mind) and no thought (in HSOM, SC mind), there is FREE (in YOU) which is beyond thought and no thought.

As there is the Finite mind and the Sub-Conscious mind, there is YOU/SELF which is beyond the F Mind and the SC Mind. We just need to KNOW YOU/FREE and ACCEPT it.

ACCEPTANCE is the SECRET.

There is a difference between the mind and YOU, so YOU are capable of turning it into the gateway to freedom. By ignorance, we take YOU as the MIND. We need to understand the difference between the MIND and YOU. Our Mind is related to desires/HC, while YOU are related to being FREE.

The interesting thing is that our HC comes to us ITSELF when we, YOU knows/becomes FREE.

So, we will know FREE in the RS now.

Let's start with FREE.

Why be FREE? Because:

1. We were born FREE, and FREE is our ETERNAL search.

2. We understand the difference between the MIND and YOU, and we know the difference between the thoughts and no thoughts/HSOM and FREE.

3. FREE is a knowing; as we usually understand the thoughts and no thoughts/HSOM, but now we know that FREE is neither a thought, nor no thought, but a KNOWING which comes afterthoughts and no thoughts.

4. FREE never means to leave, but to go to the next state in the hierarchy. So FREE never intends to leave the Mind, but to go to the next state where the mind becomes one with YOU/FREE and works better and more focused.

5. FREE is an IDEA too.

Wealth (Money + health, happiness, harmonious relationships, a harmonious life) comes to us ITSELF when YOU become FREE.

YOU–YOU are not the mind

It is self/soul, but let's call it YOU/FREE. You are related to the FREE. FREE is another name for YOU. Since we were born FREE, there is no need to create it. We have had it already, but our desires overtook our FREE. All that you have to do is to go beyond the finite mind to the SC mind, and from the SC mind to YOU, i.e., FREE. Mind (the Finite mind and the SC mind) is not YOU. YOU are not MIND; YOU are beyond MIND. Its form is silence, and it is the real knowledge.

Of the free soul who has shredded all attachment, whose mind is firmly grounded in knowledge, who acts only for sacrifice, all karma is extinguished.

- Bhagavad Gita

As a blazing fire turns its fuel to ashes, even so, the fire of Knowledge turns all actions to ashes.

- Bhagavad Gita

We created/followed HC thoughts and the HSOM, but we need not create or follow the FREE because we were born FREE. We just need to know FREE which is in our very nature. We are that, FREE. We were born FREE, but the desires overtook our FREE self, which means that the MIND overtook YOU, i.e., FREE, and then we started thinking that YOU is MIND.

Now, however, we go along preparing our HC through the Finite mind and then the SC mind and finally reach YOU, i.e., FREE. We have been moving towards FREE along with our HC. FREE is our real nature. It is not to be freshly acquired. It only comes after knowing the Finite mind and the SC. mind, i.e., after going beyond the HC thoughts chanting and then the HSOM. Know then that knowledge of YOU, i.e., FREE does not create a new being for YOU.FREE only grows us towards the FREE level 3 / HC level 3.

YOU are not MIND. We don't need to hold it or understand it. FREE is not a thought, not an HSOM (no thought). Just know it, i.e., it comes after the HSOM, but is beyond thought and HSOM (no thought). No thought is not FREE because thought (Finite mind) and no thought (the SC mind) is related with the Mind, but FREE is not related with the MIND; FREE is related with YOU; only YOU know it. The Finite mind will try to know FREE in the thought form and would try to name it, while the SC mind will try to know it in the HSOM (no thought) form, but because YOU are not the MIND, only YOU know it. YOU ACCEPT it.

Your ACCEPTANCE is the secret.

The straightforward way to know FREE is: if the Finite mind thinks of FREE as a thought and the SC mind thinks that FREE is HSOM (no thought), then it is not FREE; we are only with the MIND still (the Finite mind or the SC mind). However, only when YOU know that FREE is beyond the MIND, i.e., thought and HSOM (no thought), YOU will know it in reality and will genuinely enter the FREE. FREE is neither thought nor non-thought; FREE knows that YOU are not MIND, and that FREE comes beyond the thoughts and no thoughts stage.

YOU were FREE for a moment.

It's Momentary.

YOU moved into FREE.

Only YOU know FREE.

ONLY YOU ACCEPT FREE.

That's why we followed the HC thoughts chanting, to prepare our HC in the PS and followed the HSOM exercise in the RS to know YOU, i.e., FREE. FREE plays the RESULTS part for your HC.

Now the question is, did we know FREE? The answer is YES because you don't need to hold FREE, but just KNOW it. FREE is not creating anything new or following something, it is a knowing only, that we were born FREE and have known FREE again.

When we think of the finite mind, we call it thinking; when we don't think by the sub-conscious mind, i.e., in the HSOM exercise, we call it no thinking. There is the SC mind which doesn't think and then beyond thc no thinking, i.e., beyond the SC mind, there is FREE. Knowing it's YOU/ FREE beyond the mind (the Finite mind with thoughts and the SC mind with no thoughts) and beyond thinking and no thoughts.

Because thinking and no thinking are related to the mind and not YOU, YOU are related to FREE which is beyond thinking and no thinking. To know FREE, we need to know the Harmonious Combination thoughts chanting and the no thoughts (HSOM). FREE is beyond the HC thoughts chanting and the HSOM (no thoughts). Just know that it is not a thought, neither a non-thought; it is beyond both of them. The mind can't know FREE because the Finite mind will always try to find it in thought and the SC mind will try to see it in the HSOM (no thought). It is just YOU who knows it because YOU are not MIND (not Finite mind and not the SC mind either). YOU are beyond the Finite mind and the SC mind. Just know that YOU are not MIND, and only YOU know FREE. As there is a thought (Finite mind) and no thought (SC mind),there is FREE and YOU which are neither in the F mind nor the SC mind, but beyond both of them, so only YOU know that FREE is beyond the mind, i.e., beyond thought and no thought. FREE is neither a thought nor a no thought, but a knowing.

ACCEPTANCE is the SECRET.

Now the question in the RS is, how to remain FREE to reach the Supreme Schedule?

There is a hierarchy: Finite mind, SC mind, YOU/ FREE, the billions, the SUPREME, the Practice of Gratitude(POG). (Later, POS(Practice of Surrender).)

HC thoughts go from chanting and HSOM to FREE.

You need not follow FREE like the HC thought chanting or the HSOM, **but as soon as YOU know FREE, it turns into GRATITUDE; Gratitude for the billions and Gratitude for the SUPREME.**

Now, the HC thoughts chanting is very limited/focused on one or two thoughts, plus we have creative thoughts, and the HSOM exercise has FREE, i.e., it is with Gratitude in it.

We have selected the HC thought chanting and HSOM even after knowing FREE in the RS because being FREE is not to hold and follow, as the HC thought chanting and HDOM, but to have Gratitude and knowing the YOU/ FREE which will take us to the Supreme Schedule.

FREE plays the RESULTS part for our HC, and to remain FREE we go take refuge of the POG (the Practice of Gratitude) because YOU now see the same FREE in all the 7.4 + billion. In addition, YOU know that if YOU, i.e., FREE is so wonderful, then how wonderful would the SUPREME be, which is even beyond YOU (in the hierarchy).

All of us billions have a PARTICLE of the SUPREME, and YOU are a PARTICLE of the SUPREME in all of us billions.

Here comes the GRATITUDE for the billions and the SUPREME. If YOU are following the POG, it means that YOU are FREE, as YOU know the FREE now. YOU may again follow the selected HC thoughts/ideas in the RS, but now YOU know FREE so YOU, only YOU, know the difference between the MIND and YOU, i.e., YOU know the difference between thoughts, no thoughts and FREE. It means that YOU are FREE from the MIND because now YOU understand the difference between the MIND and YOU.

FREE never mean to leave the MIND, we still follow the HC thoughts chanting and the HSOM in the RS, but we support a few selected thoughts which makes our HC thoughts very focused and creative. Our HSOM exercise is more harmonious now too because YOU know FREE now. So, FREE never means to leave the MIND, but the MIND becomes ONE with YOU and is at its highest level of functioning. The MIND has now become CREATIVE. The BEST and the most CREATIVE thoughts and ideas now come to the MIND and are very helpful in the PLANNING of our HC.

According to the hierarchy, we go from the Mind to YOU and so on, finally reaching the POG gradually by knowing each one in the RS. This is called PERSONAL GROWTH in the RS, which is very important. There is a saying that if YOU want to grow in your HC as well as in your job, career or money and keep growing, then YOU need to build yourself personally too.

FREE can be felt/known only by YOU; it can never be understood mentally.

HC thoughts are for us in the PS, then go beyond the thoughts by HSOM (exercise; tongue curl up) and finally, beyond HSOM is to know the YOU/FREE.

The HC thought and HSOM become one with FREE. Now, MIND is energized by FREE, not by the HC thoughts and the HSOM. A knowing of which the Mind knows nothing. MIND cannot know YOU/FREE, it can only give it the name of YOU / FREE. FREE can only be known directly by YOU.

In the RS, we know that we are not Mind. The mind becomes one with the FREE/YOU in the RS, but more focused and creative now. FREE means rising above the HC thoughts and HSOM (in the RS) and not falling back to the MIND, but being with FREE.

We still use our thinking mind when needed, but in a much more focused and creative way than before. We do not need thought to know the FREE/YOU; to go to YOU from the SC mind is called FREE.As YOU know free, it turns into gratitude, gratitude for the billions and the SUPREME. Only YOU can know it and imagine, if FREE is so wonderful how much more wonderful the Supreme is (free from all), which is beyond yourself.

As YOU/Self know FREE, it turns into GRATITUDE,

Gratitude for the billions and the SUPREME, because we were FREE by birth.

We are connected with the billions and the Supreme, so FREE turns to GRATITUDE now, and YOU follow the POG in the RS. We follow the POG, thanking and accepting the billions and the Supreme, thanking & accepting for making us FREE again.

By GRATITUDE, FREE can be KNOWN and one can truly enter into FREE. Know the hierarchy from the Mind to the POG. Now from YOU/FREE, we will go to the Billions, the SUPREME and the POG. The most straightforward is the deepest, follow the POG and be free.

We billions

The Hierarchy–Mind, YOU, the Billions, the SUPREME, the POG (Practice of Gratitude), from the POG to the POS (Practice of Surrender) in the Supreme Schedule–the last and final in the hierarchy.

Let's now know the billions and the SUPREME. The SC mind listens to the voice of the billions, connects with those billions by connecting your HC plans/goals with the billions through your purpose.

We billions have desires. We are all connected with each other directly or indirectly by our desires. We all are connected, which is why our desires/HC are being fulfilled between us billions, which is why our HC is arranged between us billions. We all have desires and money is the strongest desire in today's world. However, we also desire health, happiness, a harmonious life and harmonious relationships. We are all helping each other to fulfil our desires, directly or indirectly. We all desire MONEY. Desiring money is good.

End all misconceptions about desiring money by making an HC (Aim–MONEY – PURPOSE).We are not taught well about desiring money. That is why we have misconceptions about desiring money. Money comes to those who have a desire for Money and who have made an HC. Combine your desire for money with the work you like to do the most, i.e., your aim in life and with a social motive, i.e., your ultimate aim. We make a HC of our Aim, Money and Purpose. By combining our desires with our aim and our ultimate aim, we connect ourselves with the billions. This ends all the misconceptions around desiring money.

We all can desire money. We should prepare our minds for it. We do not have to go anywhere to study it, but prepare it within our minds. We start receiving money when our mind becomes harmonious. Most of us give up the desire for money early on. This is due to the bondage (questions/worry/fear/doubts) about receiving our desire, money.

Do not give up your desire/HC. Overcome the bondage of your mind. Bondage (q/w/f/d) regarding the receiving of your desire is related to the mind only. It binds/obscures our understanding. We should end the bondage of our mind by understanding the mind. We should prepare our minds to end the bondage to make them harmonious for receiving money. We billions are making each other rich. Think of any multinational company. They are serving us billions, and we billions are buying their products, and thus these companies are receiving large amounts of money. Because they have connected themselves with us, the billions, by their desire for money. Understand it well.

Simply, we are connected with our family and we desire just as much money which is enough for our family, so we make the smallest HC. We have within us the feelings/ideas for our family. However, those who connect themselves with the billions by the biggest HC combine their desire of the biggest money with the biggest aim and their ultimate aim. They have the feelings/ideas of the billions within them, which help them receive large amounts of money for their biggest HC.

The effort is more or less the same for those who desire big money and those who desire little money. Perhaps those who desire little money are making more effort than those who desire big money. Only those who desire big money make a little more effort for preparing within his/her mind. This is not taught in schools.

Those who become billionaires prepare for it within their minds. Some of them have even written about it. Now you will be told very clearly what has not been explained before.

By birth, we were already connected with the Billions, and now after Knowing FREE, we are connected with the Billions again. By connecting with the billions with our HC, we grow the HC level 2, and by connecting with the billions in the POG (Practice of Gratitude), YOU grow the FREE level 2.

The Supreme -

Fix your mind on me, be devoted to me, offer service to me, bow down to me, and you shall certainly reach me. I promise you because you are my very dear friend.

—Bhagavad Gita, Chapter 18, Verse 65

There is only ONE supreme. The supreme is working harmoniously within all of us billions.

The Supreme is working harmoniously in ALL of us billions in two ways:

1. Through our minds;
2. Beyond our minds.

1. Through Our Minds:

The supreme is linked through our minds. Knowing FREE makes our minds harmonious with the SUPREME. When our minds become harmonious, we have harmonious feelings of gratitude for the SUPREME, and we start enjoying life to its fullness. We have gratitude towards the SUPREME, and as an ultimate gratitude to the SUPREME; we have gratitude for all of us billions.

2. Beyond Our Minds:

The SUPREME makes arrangements for our HC for us billions and arranges between us billions. The Supreme gives us all our HC in REALITY. How the supreme does it, is beyond our minds. We cannot understand it, but what we can understand is that the Supreme has made arrangements for all of us billions. This much understanding is enough for us because the more we try to understand, the greater will be the Acceptance and deeper will be the Gratitude for the Supreme. All the greats of the past and present accept this one thing that there is one power which guides all of us billions. The harmonious feelings for the SUPREME make our mind harmonious. Thus, we have great HC thoughts and ideas, and our Gratitude grows.

We thank and accept the Supreme in our Gratitude for the SUPREME. By thanking and accepting the billions, we pay the ultimate gratitude to the SUPREME. By thanking and accepting the supreme, we gain a secure understanding of having HC RESULTS and HC related things, i.e., health, happiness, harmonious relationships, and a harmonious life in abundance. We start enjoying our HC and other HC related things in abundance, and the REALITY starts enjoying our HC too, while the HC related things are in abundance and REALITY is a pre-RESULT atmosphere before reaching the Supreme Schedule.

The Supreme is beyond our mind, yet we are linked with the Supreme through our minds. We understand a little about the harmonious way of working of the Supreme through our minds only. Moreover, we understand how miraculous the Supreme is then, which is beyond our minds. According to Hindu philosophy, it is believed that one eternal being exists and connects us all; this we call the

SUPREME. One in all and all in one. The SUPREME and YOU are in some sense the same.

In Hinduism, bliss/enjoyment is conceived as the state of total union with the SUPREME, in which YOU are completely merged. There are chances that EGO {YOU = Ego (a tiny part) + FREE (the major part)} comes in to make you feel that YOU are FREE now and that YOU can get all the results on your own, but YOU should know that ONLY the SUPREME gives/makes our HC in REALITY. When YOU ACCEPT, your EGO turns into GRATITUDE for the SUPREME. The SUPREME gives/makes our HC in reality and the SUPREME only needs your GRATITUDE. He who dedicates (not leaving) all his actions (physically and mentally) to the Supreme, acts as if no effort is done in real.

The POG makes the SUPREME give us our HC harmoniously. Give your Gratitude to the billions and the SUPREME from all of us billions. THANK and ACCEPT the billions and the SUPREME in the POG, daily morning to evening. THANK and ACCEPT for making YOU FREE, for already having given you your HC.As you are already living harmoniously with your HC, this is the Gratitude for the Billions and the SUPREME.

By Gratitude, YOU/self knows the SUPREME (free from all) as seeming to possess the functions of the senses. It is devoid of all the senses. It touches naught, upholds all. Having no sins, it experiences the sins. Without all beings, yet within; immovable yet moving, so subtle that it cannot be perceived; so far and yet so near it is. It is the SUPREME.

Undivided, it seems to subsist divided in all beings; light of all lights, it is said to be beyond darkness; it is knowledge, the object of knowledge, to be gained only by knowledge; it is seated in the hearts of all.

- Bhagavad Gita

THE POG (THE PRACTICE OF GRATITUDE)

By thanking and accepting the billions

in the POG,YOU stay FREE by following the POG.

The Practice of Gratitude makes the Supreme harmoniously work for your HC and HC related things. Just follow the Practice of Gratitude every day after waking up in the morning and before sleeping in the night –

(You may have according to your belief in the POG).

"We thank you billions, and we accept you billions, and we thank you Supreme, and we accept you Supreme."

1. Thanking and accepting for preparing in our HC and for great values,

2. Thanking and accepting the billions for connecting for our HC,

3. Thanking and accepting the supreme in advance for giving us our HC in reality and giving us in reality until the last,

4. Thanking and accepting the POG for making the supreme harmoniously work for our HC PLANS,

5. Thanking and accepting the POG for making us FREE.

Thanking and accepting for your HC and HC related things in the POG, gratitude creates the fullness of life, makes YOU and your HC harmonious.

We were born FREE, we were ONE with the billions and

the SUPREME, and were full of GRATITUDE. It is our NATURE. We have already had it. Include all things which are helping in your HC in the Practice of Gratitude. The Supreme wants our Gratitude and Surrender only. By the POG, we have connected with the Supreme again. Connected means in an easy way by having gone from YOU and the billions to the SUPREME, by the POG.

Present all your EFFORTS (physical and mental) to the SUPREME.

It feels as if tons of weight has been shed from your mind and YOU.

Follow the POG, thanking and accepting the SUPREME for making you EASY with all the ACTION (plan/goals) and for making YOU FREE.

YOU have connected with the SUPREME by the POG.

Know that the SUPREME gives YOU your HC PLANS in reality (only the SUPREME turns your HC in reality), but it is the POG which makes the SUPREME harmonious to give YOU your HC PLANS in reality. The SUPREME only wants your GRATITUDE for it.

So, it is the POG which makes the SUPREME harmonious, to give you your HC PLANS in reality. YOU have gone to the SUPREME by the POG. The POG has made YOU stay FREE by following the POG, YOU have gone next to the POG in the hierarchy.

Now YOU are ready to enter the Supreme Schedule.

Know the hierarchy of the finite mind: SC mind–YOU–the billions–the SUPREME–the POG (the POS).

YOU become FREE by ACCEPTANCE. ACCEPTANCE is the secret. Accepting that YOU are beyond the Mind and

ACCEPTING that only the SUPREME can give you HC in REALITY.

YOU are a PARTICLE of the SUPREME. This PARTICLE is in all of us billions.

Like our mind has two parts, the conscious mind and the subconscious mind, you also have two parts -

1. Ego (Minor part of YOU)

2. FREE (Major part of YOU)

The EGO has YEARNINGS for the HC and has EGO that it may get our HC in reality. Living every day with ALL our HC goals, we have YEARNINGS.

YEARNINGS are of the HC RESULTS and receiving HC related thing such as health, happiness, harmonious relationships, a harmonious life every day. Understand that RESULTS/Receiving is continuous and between receiving one HC goal and the next, one has a creating process. Receiving our desired goal is a momentary point for us.

After receiving the desired goal, it becomes a part of it to receive the next goal and so on. With one HC plan complete, we move on to complete all the plans of our HC. YEARNINGS have a lot of ENERGY; YEARNINGS are also a sign that we are going close to the Supreme Schedule.

YOU may have difficulty in handling these yearnings. But these yearnings become harmonious by the POG.

FREE is filled with gratitude for the billions and the Supreme. As the EGO ACCEPTS, only the SUPREME gives the HC in reality, the EGO becomes ONE with the FREE.

The SUPREME harmoniously gives HC in REALITY when YOU become FREE from all. The SUPREME is harmoniously working for our HC.

FREE is already accepting the billions and the SUPREME in the practice of Gratitude.

Present ALL (from all HC effort and ALL HC) to the SUPREME and be EASY.

(HC effort–from following an HC thought to following an HSOM, plans/goals, is an HC effort)

As the mind has bondage, the bondage of YOU keeps you with the HC efforts, thus not allowing you to go to the next step, i.e., to the SS for RESULTS. By presenting your HC efforts and the HC to the Supreme, and by following the POG, we are ready to enter the Supreme Schedule.

Follow the POG: Give your gratitude to the billions and the Supreme. The Practice of Gratitude makes the SUPREME harmoniously give you your HC in REALITY. YOU have the KNOWING now. Your ACCEPTANCE is the secret. You would ACCEPT it. YOU have already received your HC, before you have them in the Supreme Schedule, by the POG. YOU accept that YOU have already received all your HC by the POG through us billions and the SUPREME. YOU accept the POG.

Your HC and HC related things, i.e., health, happiness, harmonious relationships and a harmonious life come to you by THEMSELVES (by the POG, through us billions and the SUPREME) in REALITY, now harmoniously.

YOU live harmoniously with your HC after receiving all the HC in reality. YOU accept that YOU have already lived harmoniously after receiving your HC.

Receiving Schedule Heads

1. THE POG

The Receiving Schedule is headed by the POG and has six heads. Follow the POG, morning to evening daily, after waking and before sleeping, thanking and accepting the billions, the SUPREME and the POG for making your HC harmonious and for knowing the hierarchy.

2. HSOM Exercise

Very selected HC thoughts chanting. Follow the HSOM exercise every day in the morning and the evening, for 15–20 minutes.

But the man who revels in Atman, who is content in Atman and who is satisfied only with Atman, for him no action exists.

- Bhagavad Gita

Tranquil in spirit, free from fear, steadfast in the vow of Brahmacharya, holding his mind in control, the yogi should sit, with all his thoughts on me, absorbed in me.

- Bhagavad Gita

3. Brahmacharya/Love

Brahmacharya (usually translated as 'celibacy') means not only sexual continence but also the observance of all the cardinal vows for the attainment of Brahman.

- Bhagavad Gita

Free thyself from the pairs of opposites, abide in the eternal truth, scorn to gain or guard anything, remain the master of thy soul.

- Bhagavad Gita

By one's Self should one raise oneself, and not allow oneself to fall; for Atman (Self) alone is the friend of self, and Self alone is self's foe.

- Bhagavad Gita

Love makes us harmonious. Love is the motivational force, which keeps us following the HC plan/Goals, every day. Love is spiritual.

Have a firm understanding of having HC RESULTS and HC related things in abundance in the SS. Make your understanding more and more secure every day by following the Receiving Schedule. Have confidence, the skill of decision-making, definiteness of plans. One should plan his work and work his plan, a pleasing personality, sympathy and understanding, mastery of detail and taking full responsibility.

Following the RS, and the HC PLAN shows our Gratitude for the greats of the PAST and PRESENT. Develop your personality. Have a relaxing time on the weekend. On weekends do nothing, think nothing.

Knowledge of YOU/FREE makes our HC harmonious. As the fire consumes the fuel, in the flame of Knowledge of YOU/FREE, the embers of action burn to ashes. There is nothing in the world so purifying as Knowledge of YOU / FREE. When the Mind, wholly centred in the YOU and fixed on his HC plans/Goals, then YOU have already done that YOU need to do.

The mind is fickle and exceedingly difficult to restrain, but with constant practice and Gratitude, it can be done. Follow the POG, be kind and compassionate, unselfishness, without pride, equable in pleasure and pain, and forgiving, always contented, resolute, with mind and reason, all efforts dedicated to the SUPREME. Humility, sincerity, harmlessness, forgiveness, rectitude, steadfastness, the absence of pride, Unswerving devotion, love for solitude, knowledge of YOU/FREE and pondering over the lessons of the great Truth – this is Knowledge, all else ignorance. He who can see the Supreme Lord in all beings, have the Emotional intelligence to regulate yourselves, interact with other people in everyday situations.

Handle criticism empathically and improve those areas. Handle criticism without denial, blame, excuses or anxiety. Follow the Brahmacharya organized sex activity monthly or half-monthly, rest all the things as told in the Preparing Schedule about Brahmacharya means about diet, rest, etc.

Whatever the best man does, is also done by other men, the example he sets, the world follows.

- Bhagavad Gita

Fearlessness, purity of heart, steadfastness in jnana and yoga — knowledge and action, beneficence, self-restraint, sacrifice, spiritual study, austerity, and uprightness. Non-violence, truth, slowness to wrath, the spirit of dedication, serenity, aversion to slander, tenderness to all that lives, freedom from greed, gentleness, modesty, freedom from levity. Spiritedness, forgiveness, fortitude, purity, freedom from ill-will and arrogance — these the divine heritage. The divine heritage makes for Freedom

- Bhagavad Gita

Victuals that add to one's years, vitality, strength, health, happiness, and appetite; are savory, rich, substantial and inviting, are dear to the sattvika.

- Bhagavad Gita

That sacrifice is sattvika, which is willingly offered as a duty without desire for fruit and according to the rule. Homage to the gods, to gurus and wise men; cleanliness, uprightness, Brahmacharya, and non-violence —these constitute austerity of the body.

- Bhagavad Gita

Words that cause no hurt are genuinely loving, and helpful and spiritual study constitute austerity of speech.

- Bhagavad Gita

Serenity, benignity, silence, self-restraint, and purity of the spirit — these constitute austerity of the mind.

- Bhagavad Gita

This threefold austerity practiced in perfect faith by men not desirous of fruit, and disciplined, is said to be sattvika.

- Bhagavad Gita

4. Constantly Practice

Let not thy motive be the fruit of action, nor shouldn't thou desire to avoid action.

- Bhagavad Gita

Never does man enjoy freedom from action by not undertaking action, nor does he attain that freedom by mere renunciation of action. For none ever remains inactive even for a moment.

- Bhagavad Gita

Do thou thy allotted task; for action is superior to inaction; with inaction, even life's ordinary course is not possible.

- Bhagavad Gita

By continually applying HC thoughts/Ideas on your HC PLAN/Goals, every day you become richer. The more you believe it, the more your subconscious will become harmonious. Join group related to your HC or join a business group. Meet regularly. Have the cooperation of other people; work on your Plans/Goals. Go for a new plan if the current plan is not satisfying. Until you find a plan that works. Have persistence and continuously work on HC plans/Goals and grow yourself and your product.

FOCUS ON OPPORTUNITIES. Write to people in higher networks. Join a business group can do the same thing. Be among people who are already successful in the areas you want to succeed and study them. Gain knowledge from them, listen to the great speeches. Use the experience in your HC plans/Goals.

Have Great IDEAS, use the moral of IDEAS in your daily life. You are moving towards the Supreme Schedule, and in the Supreme Schedule, you have resulted of your HC in ABUNDANCE. Build a list of all the things from where your HC RESULTS can come. Grow yourself into a successful person. Grow FREE level 2 and HC level 2; again, your HC level is merely a reflection of your FREE level. FREE level is the root of your HC level, so grow from FREE level 2/HC level 2 to towards FREE level 3/ HC level 3. Slow and steady practice to be RICH.

Constant practice and constant efforts, persistence are ideal tools for it. Act thou, without attachment, steadfast in Yoga, even-minded in success and failure.

- Bhagavad Gita

5. VISUALISING HC PLAN/Goals -

Every day in the evening, have some spare time for visualizing your HC plan/goals.

Visualize your current year's plan and the next year's plan. Visualize that you are having your current year plan and you are starting your next year plan. Visualize your goal repeatedly. See it in your mind's eye as though it were already a reality. The more clear and vivid the mental picture of your goal, the easier it will come into your life. Feel good as that you would have if you achieved your HC plans/goal. Feel good as if it is bringing your goal into reality. Accept that you are moving toward your goal and it is moving toward you.

Create a Goal that is clear to your subconscious mind. Plan or plans would come to you itself. Give Gratitude and work on these Plans by visualizing HC. Be specific in your visualization. Make the image clear; hold it firmly in mind. Therefore, you are to picture in your mind what you want and do it daily until the picture becomes clear and do the visualization wherever you feel relax.

6. TIME

Our HC takes time and becoming rich too takes time, but we are in much better in Preparing Schedule and Receiving Schedule working on our HC, and we will have RESULTS in ABUNDANCE in the Supreme Schedule. Take care of the time, divide your HC plan (yearly) into months. Make the daily schedule and Act on it and go to sleep on time.

Health, Happiness, Harmonious relationships, harmonious life and Wealth (Money + net worth) is called RICHES, and all of them are in ABUNDANCE,

Think about them in the PS, and you know them in the Receiving Schedule and get them in the SS.

It means you will have them in ABUNDANCE in the Supreme Schedule.

THE Receiving Schedule:

1. The POG - following the POG daily, after waking in the morning and before sleeping in the evening.
2. Sub-Conscious Mind–HSOM By daily chanting in your mind. "We billions are receiving money now." and by HSOM ex. 15-20 minutes in the morning and the evening
3. Brahmacharya/Love
4. Always apply your thoughts to your HC Plan/Goals
5.Visualize your HC plan/Goals
6. TIME

HC PLAN FOR THE CURRENT YEAR-

What do you want to do this year/how much money do you want to have this year/what is your social motive for this year?

HC PLAN FOR NEXT YEAR-

Your next year HC plan should follow the current year.

Make your HC for ten years of the RS, and then divide it into yearly, two years, five years.

Make rough HC plans for 20 years and 40 years to until the end of the SS.

ACCEPTANCE is the SECRET.

The essence of the RS is to know the hierarchy and to move up from mind to the POG, to present our all efforts (from HC Plans/Goals) to the SUPREME. So that we may move from efforts to the RESULTS in the Supreme Schedule.

Following the HC Plans/Goals in the RS and by knowing the hierarchy from Mind, YOU, the billions, the Supreme to the POG, in the RS, we enter the SS. Following the POG, thanking and accepting the billions and the Supreme for making YOU/FREE.

Only the POG makes YOU stay FREE as well as the POG gives YOU a gratitude state for all billions and the SUPREME, for the whole day. This Gratitude state for all billions and the SUPREME is harmoniously working for your HC plans/goals as well as is the refuge for YOU/SELF.

We are ready to enter the SS; from FREE level 2/HC level 2 to FREE level 3/HC level 3 YOU stay FREE by the POG. In the SS, YOU will be FREE from all. YOU will be just a witness/spectator the RESULTS part for HC as well as HC related things Wealth, Health, Happiness, Harmonious relationships, Harmonious life will be done for YOU, YOU will make no effort in real in the SS.

Let's enter the SS. As FREE turns into Gratitude in the RS, Gratitude turns into SURRENDER, in the SS. And still if there remains any bondage, then all the remaining bondage would be overcome by the POS (The Practice of Surrender) in the SS.

Equipped with the purified knowledge of the YOU/FREE, living in solitude, spare in diet, restrained in body, speech, and mind, absorbed in HSOM exercise, without pride, violence, arrogance, lust, wrath, having shed all sense of EGO and at peace with YOU/FREE. YOU are fit to become ONE with the SUPREME. ONE with the SUPREME and at peace with YOU/FREE. Now YOU doesn't think of RESULTS but ACTS, holding all beings alike YOU give your Gratitude to the Billions and the Supreme.

By Gratitude, YOU realizes in truth how beautiful the Supreme is and having known the Supreme, YOU SURRENDER to the SUPREME, in the Practice of SURRENDER (The POS) and enters in the Supreme Schedule.

4

The Supreme Schedule (SS) (40+ to the last)

Free level 3/HC level 3

The Preparing Schedule (PS) is mainly for preparing our Harmonious Combination (HC). The Receiving Schedule (RS) is about knowing YOU/FREE and for HC plans/goals.

The Supreme Schedule (SS) is for receiving the HC RESULTS and HC related things in ABUNDANCE and following the POS (Practice of Surrender).

The hardest part of the Harmonious Combination is the RESULTS (let us call them HC Results), that will be done by the POS (Practice of Surrender). The POS is the SECRET of SECRETS. Those who have known the Receiving Schedule have now entered the Supreme Schedule. Those who followed consciously or unconsciously the Receiving Schedule, may just read/know the RS to enter the SS. The Supreme Schedule is a manifestation of the Preparing Schedule and the Receiving Schedule.

We all reach the Supreme Schedule. All those who have already reached the SS have the supreme bliss and the HC RESULTS (+ HC Results related things) in Abundance and in REALITY. Those who were already in the SS, have already had the HC RESULTS (+ HC Results associated things) in Abundance and in REALITY.

Those who are of 40 years of age or more may straight away follow the Supreme Schedule. Be specific about your HC Result now; the POS is doing all the HC RESULTS part.

Action alone is thy province, not the RESULTS.

When a man starves his senses, the objects of those senses disappear for him, but not the yearning for them; the yearning departs when he beholds the Supreme.

- Bhagavad Gita

By offering the worship of his duty to Him who is the moving spirit of all beings and by whom all this is pervaded, man wins perfection.

- Bhagavad Gita

Of the enlightened ever attached to me in single-minded devotion, is the best for the enlightened; I am exceedingly dear, and he is dear to me.

- Bhagavad Gita

Living in solitude, spare in diet, restrained in speech, body, and mind, ever absorbed in dhyana yoga, anchored in dispassion. Without pride, violence, arrogance, lust, wrath, possession, having shed all sense of 'mine' and at peace with himself, he is fit to become one with Brahmaan. I will now declare to thee, who art uncensorious, this mysterious knowledge, together with discriminative learning, knowing which thou shalt be released from all. This is the king of sciences, the king of mysteries, pure and sovereign, capable of direct comprehension, the essence of dharma, accessible to practice, changeless.

- Bhagavad Gita

Whatever thou doest, whatever thou eats, whatever thou offers as sacrifice or gift, whatever austerity thou dost perform, dedicate all to me. So doing thou shalt be released from the bondage of action.

- Bhagavad Gita

FREE turns into GRATITUDE, and Gratitude into SURRENDER by the Practice of Surrender.

Faith and gratitude are born from surrender. YOU were born FREE of all. You were one with the BILLIONS and the SUPREME. YOU were FULL of GRATITUDE. FREE turns into GRATITUDE in the Receiving Schedule (RS), and Gratitude turns into SURRENDER in the Supreme Schedule (SS).

The Preparing Schedule (PS) preparing our HC, and the Receiving Schedule (RS) receiving knowledge of our HC/ FREE is a continuous process, but the Supreme Schedule (SS) has mainly the HC RESULTS. The PS and the RS take us to the HC RESULTS in the SS, as well as towards health, happiness, harmonious relationships and a harmonious life in ABUNDANCE. In the SS, YOU are not making any effort in real.

GITA Verse–Action alone is thy province, not the results!

YOU are not making any effort in real, just act in your capacity every day for your HC. In the SS, there are HC

RESULTS of your HC & HC Results related things in reality and abundance.

HC RESULTS mean the HC RESULTS of receiving +maintaining, sustaining, and completing your HC Results and HC Result related things, i.e., health, happiness, harmonious relationships and a harmonious life till the last, i.e., till 80+.

It's a bigger version of results. We usually think of results as something that can be RECEIVED. For example, you want to be rich and if you get 1 million for your PRODUCT, that is just receiving. What is more important is to STAY prosperous, grow RICH and keep developing your PRODUCT until YOU get your written net worth until the last, i.e., until 80+. Similarly, if you want to be healthy, it is good to have a healthy body now, but it is more important to stay healthy until last, i.e., 80+.

So, the bigger version of RESULTS is RECEIVE + maintain, sustain, and complete your HC Results until the last. Receiving is just a part of the whole HC RESULTS.

RESULTS = RECEIVING + maintaining, sustaining and completing your HC until the last. This is the BIGGER version of the HC RESULTS, but the HC RESULTS part is not yours. It will be played for YOU. You have already gone through the Preparing Schedule (PS) and the Receiving Schedule (RS). YOU are in the Supreme Schedule (SS) now. Have the supreme bliss, i.e., bliss in every moment.

Know the hierarchy again: Finite mind–subconscious mind–YOU–the billions–The SUPREME–The POG (The POS).

YOU are behind the billions, the SUPREME and the POG. As in the Supreme Schedule (SS), YOU grow the

FREE level 3, YOU go ahead from the billions to the SUPREME, then to the POS (Practice of Surrender), and ultimately become ONE with them by SURRENDER.

That is called FREE level 3, that is to grow YOU to go ahead from YOU to the POS and entirely become ONE with them by SURRENDER.

The enlightened may not confuse the mind of the unenlightened who are attached to action; instead, must he perform all activities unattached and thus encourage them to do likewise, but unattached should the enlightened man act, with a desire for the welfare of humanity.

- Bhagavad Gita

One who thinks about surrender, speaks about surrender and hears about surrender, spends one's life revelling (delight) in surrender all the time.

In the state of surrender, YOU become very light and easy.

Surrender is simple, where YOU experience the rhythm and flow of life.

Surrendermeansunderstandingthehierarchy.Acceptance moves YOU from the mind and thus reconnects you with the billions and the Supreme and with the POS. Surrender is the highest in the hierarchy. Surrender to reach the highest level in the hierarchy by becoming one with all the heads of the hierarchy. The essence of the SS is SURRENDER. Following the POS raises FREE from all–free level 3/ HC level 3. As only YOU know FREE, after chanting (thoughts) and HSOM (no thoughts), only YOU know FREE at all. Simply understand that after surrendering all my HC results and myself to my POS, the POS makes me free from all.

Our non-surrender of HC Results and non-surrender of YOU/FREE overtook our FREE from all. All that YOU/ FREE have to do is to take the refuge of SURRENDER of your POS. We created/followed HC thoughts and followed HSOM, but we need not generate or support the 'FREE from all'. We just need to know FREE from all. The straightforward way to know FREE from all is by surrender, i.e., by following the POS.

Its the TIME NOW for RECEIVING all your HC Results in the Supreme Schedule. Your PART is to RECEIVE only; all HC Results come to YOU themselves by the POS. Your part is to be entirely READY to RECEIVE all your HC results in REALITY, and NOW. Many have received, many are receiving, and many will receive their HC RESULTS by the POS in reality in the Supreme Schedule.

Have a dominant desire to RECEIVE all your HC RESULTS by the POS in REALITY now. In the PS and the RS, YOU had a dominant desire for preparing you HC in the PS, and getting the self-knowledge in the RS and prepared for 30 years. Now until the last, in the Supreme Schedule, YOU should be ready to have a dominant desire to receive all your HC Results by the POS in REALITY now.

Surrender yourself and all your HC Results in the POS, morning/evening daily, after waking & before sleeping, two times a day. Give your complete surrendering bow to the Supreme, the billions and the POS, in the POS.

RESULTS = Receiving, Sustaining, Maintaining and Completing all your HC Results.

Before giving all my HC Results till the last, my POS makes MYSELF free from all in REAL, i.e., gives

MYSELF the knowing/understanding of my POS and fills MYSELF with complete surrender for my POS.

Let's start with the simple POS -

Following my POS, morning/evening daily, after waking & before sleeping, two times.

The POS -

"I and my family surrender to you, the billions.

We billions Surrender to you, the SUPREME.

We billions surrender to you, the POS."

Gita Verse - Knowledge is the best surrender.

Surrender your Receiving Schedule (RS) knowledge, i.e., YOU/FREE, in the POS. After surrendering YOU/FREE and all your HC Results to the POS, the POS will make YOU free from all. As only YOU know free, just know that after surrendering YOU/FREE and all your HC Results to the POS, the POS will make you free from all, this is FREE level 3/HC level 3.

Acceptance is the secret.

The Practice of Surrender is the secret of secrets.

When YOU surrender YOU/FREE,

the POG (Practice of Gratitude) turns into the POS (Practice of Surrender).

There is following of the POS is in the Supreme Schedule and particular HC thoughts chanting about the POS.

1. The HC thoughts, feelings, ideas, plans, knowing is coming directly after following the POS now and these HC thoughts, feelings, ideas, plans and understanding

which is coming directly from the Practice of Surrender (POS) is much creative than your mind. So, surrender your HC thoughts chanting and the HSOM

2. If YOU chant the HC thoughts (Finite mind) about the Preparing Schedule and the Receiving Schedule, and follow HSOM (subconscious mind) of the Receiving Schedule, it means that the Mind and YOU are still there in the PS and RS, and not with your HC results in the Supreme Schedule. Mind and YOU are in the PS and the RS actively preparing and receiving knowledge; but in the Supreme Schedule, it's all about HC Results. This is the difference between the PS, the RS and the SS. YOU chant, but only the particular HC thoughts, mainly the POS thoughts, and YOU follow the HSOM but of the POS only.

3. The Mind, YOU, the billions and the SUPREME have become ONE with the POS, after following the POS.

4. FREE is beyond HC thoughts and NO thoughts are FREE, as it turns into Gratitude as soon as YOU know FREE. Gratitude turns into Surrender more quickly as YOU surrender FREE in the Practice of Surrender (POS).

FREE and Gratitude become one and enter the POS.

In the POS, give your respectful bow to the billions, the Supreme and the POS.

I am free from all by the POS; I am ready to receive ALL the HC RESULT NOW by the POS in REALITY.

There are two parts of getting READY –

1. Make yourself ready/prepared for the HC/Free–by the Preparing Schedule and the Receiving Schedule.

2. Get ready to receive all your HC Results NOW.

NOW, my part is to be ready to RECEIVE all my HC RESULTS by the POS in REALITY.

1. THE POS makes me free from all in the Supreme Schedule to RECEIVE all my HC RESULTS in REALITY NOW.

2. After having followed the Preparing Schedule (PS) and the Receiving Schedule (RS) for around 30 years, prepared the HC and having the knowledge of SELF/ YOU, the POS makes me free from all in the Supreme Schedule to RECEIVE all my HC RESULTS by the POS in REALITYNOW.

1. Now in the Supreme Schedule, I'm 40+, having only one desire–to receive all my HC Results.

2. In the Supreme Schedule, the TIME NOW is only to RECEIVE all my HC RESULTS by the POS in REALITY NOW. Just the POS makes me free from all to RECEIVE all my HC RESULTS in the REALITY NOW.

3. Add TIME NOW to create only one desire, to RECEIVE all my HC RESULTS by the POS in REALITY and ABUNDANCE.

Clear your **WHAT, WHY, HOW & WHEN.** This is the HC level 3/FREE level 3.

1. What – What do you want NOW (your HC result NOW);

2. Why – Your purpose for your HC Result NOW;

3. When – NOW;

4. How – Belief/the POS.

5. What–What do you want NOW (your HC result NOW); HC Result NOW means the HC Results which YOU want NOW.

Write down your HC Results NOW with the date-

i)

ii)

iii)

iv)

1. Why–

Your purpose for your HC Result NOW. Why do you want your HC Result NOW and all your HC Result NOW? Your objective should be clear for your HC Result NOW and all your HC Result NOW.

2. When–

When to get my HC Result NOW. Let's go to the deepest NOW/timeless NOW from NOW.

NOW is a small drop of the deepest NOW/timeless NOW. Now has YEARNINGS as well as some bondage, i.e., doubt, worry, fear, and questions.

NOW is born from timelessness/Deepest Now. If NOW is so great, how miraculous would deepest NOW/Timeless NOW/no time be?

YOU/FREE now want to keep attached with your HC Result NOW. Self/YOU intend to use all your energy, knowledge, and understanding to receive your HC Results NOW, goal NOW itself.

YOU/SELF/FREE have nothing to do with the HC Results NOW because RESULTS part is not your part.

It's your POS (Practice Of Surrender) part. This is the deepest NOW/timeless NOW. YOU become utterly passive for your HC Results NOW. My POS becomes active entirely for my HC results NOW part.

3. This is the Deepest NOW/Timeless NOW.

TIME itself doesn't exist; TIME exists when you relate things to it or where YOU are. If YOU connect time with the mind, you are in the past or the present. When you combine time to YOU, YOU are in the NOW/free/with your HC Results NOW. When YOU relate TIME with my POS, YOU are with FREE from all in the real/deepest NOW/timeless NOW/timelessness.

Often YOU may get misunderstood as a higher state to timelessness, that's why YOU want to attach with NOW only. Thus, you don't want to leave NOW because YOU/Self thinks that by leaving NOW, YOU/Self would leave all your HC Result NOW. Mind has bondage about the HC. Similarly, YOU have bondage about the HC Results NOW.

However, after following my POS, YOU understand Deepest Now and understand that Deepest Now is a higher state than NOW. NOW is born from Deepest Now/timelessness. The deepest NOW is my POS.

After following my POS, it's my POS (the deepest NOW/timeless NOW) which is the easiest way to go from NOW to Deepest Now .

My POS is related to time (NOW) as well as with Deepest Now .

As for WHAT & WHY, they are closely related and complete each other. Similarly, WHEN & HOW are closely related and complete each other.

4. HOW: Belief/the POS –

How will YOU get your HC Results NOW and all your HC Results NOW.

Let's clear HOW–Know how YOU got your previous HC Results/Goals–faith and gratitude are born of surrender.

My POS already gave me before -

1. Gave me my.........in the year................................

2. Gave me my......... in the year...............................

3. Gave me my......... in the year...............................

4. Gave me my......... in the year...............................

5. Gave me my......... in the year...............................

6. Gave me my......... in the year...............................

7. Gave me just one year before...................................

8. Giving me NOW...

Receiving is just a small part of the Results.

RESULTS = receiving, sustaining, maintaining and completing all my HC Results NOW. Collecting my HC Results NOW...............US $.

Follow my POS now. Before you start following my POS, know/understand that my POS has these five parts –

1.Surrendering to my POS

2.Chanting my POS

3.Visualization

4.Surrender-ness

5.Talking with my POS

1. Surrendering to my POS –

Surrender your HC Results NOW and all your HC Results NOW to my POS.

2. Chanting my POS –

It's my POS. It's all by (following) my POS.

3. Visualization –

How my HC Results NOW and all my HC Results NOW are received by my POS, visualize them.

4. Surrender-ness –

After visualization, pause for a few minutes, no chanting; it's surrender-ness.

5. Talking with my POS –

Talk with my POS, ask my POS.

All these five points come in following my POS. Following my POS – morning/evening daily, two times, after waking & before sleeping, until the last. Early morning is the best time, and before 10 PM is the best time at night.

Starting with any of your last HC Results which you have already received, recently or before. Visualize how that HC Result came to you and how you are doing well with it and how it happened like a miracle. Then completely surrender and bow to my POS for already giving me that HC Result.

Surrender your HC Result NOW............$, to the POS and give a complete surrendering bow to the POS for already giving me this HC Result NOW.

A complete surrendering bow to you, my POS, by myself, for already having given me my HC result NOW, and for already giving me all my HC Results NOW. Our families provide a complete surrendering bow to you, my BILLIONS, our families love you, my BILLIONS.

WE BILLIONS give a complete surrendering bow to you, my SUPREME;

WE BILLIONS love you, my SUPREME;

WE BILLIONS give a full surrendering bow to you, my POS;

WE BILLIONS love you, my POS.

Pause then for some moments and chant in your mind– It's my POS. It's all by (following) my POS (10 minutes), then visualize how this HC Result NOW (............$) will come to YOU as per your plan by my POS. During visualization, feel and react as if you are receiving your HC Result NOW. Then pause for some moments and chant in your mind – It's my POS. It's all by my POS (10-20 times).

Chant my POS joyfully, moving your head left and right. Then visualize all your HC Results NOW, one by one, receiving them. Thus, my POS has completed/received all my HC Results.

Then surrender-ness (5-8 minutes–no chanting): Surrender-ness is the complete surrendering bow to my POS. Then talk with my POS–If YOU want to ask anything, YOU ask my POS. My POS told me, I'm talking with you, NOW.

Here, it completes following my POS. After surrendering all my HC Results NOW, two times in the morning/evening, daily, after waking up& before sleeping. Observe my POS that it is working harmoniously for my HC Results NOW and for all my HC Results NOW, for receiving, sustaining, maintaining and completing all my HC Results NOW, till the very last.

Time to time, Self/YOU will try to attach with my HC Results, i.e., Self/YOU will try to say that YOU can't get all your HC results (but the RESULTS part belongs only to my POS, not Self/YOU). Time to time, the Self/YOU will try to create bondage (questions, worry, doubt, fear) about my HC Results NOW and for all my HC Results NOW too.

YOU/Self should know/understand that the RESULTS part belongs to my POS. YOU/Self might want to attach with the HC results again in your SS (40+ to 80+; 40 years). Self/YOU should know/understand that there is a higher hierarchy, i.e., we billions/my Supreme/my POS, i.e., Self/ YOU should complete the hierarchy, i.e., to go to my POS.

How many years and births do YOU/Self need to understand that after surrendering all your HC Results and yourself, the POS harmoniously works for all your HC Results and yourself till the last!

The man of faith who, scorning not, will but listen to it — even he shall be released and will go to the happy worlds of men of virtuous deeds.

- Bhagavad Gita

Hast thou heard this with a concentrated mind? Has thy delusion born of ignorance been destroyed, Arjuna said: Thanks to thy grace, my delusion is destroyed, my understanding has returned. I stand secure, my doubts all dispelled.

- Bhagavad Gita

For that, Self/YOU should know my SS as well as my POS schedule (afterlife). Let's be more clear of HOW by my POS schedule (afterlife).

There are five schedules in our life –

1. The Supreme Schedule: The SS (0-14 years of age) - Free, one with the Supreme, full of Gratitude- FREE level 3 / HC level 3

2. The Preparing Schedule: The PS (14 - 30 years of age) - Mainly about Aim/Preparing our HC - Free level 1 / HC level 1

3. The Receiving Schedule: The RS (30 - 40 years of age) - Mainly about the Knowledge of the FREE-HC and getting READY for RESULTS - Free level 2 / HC level 2

4. The Supreme Schedule: The SS (40+ - till last 80+) - Mainly consists of RECEIVING our HC / RESULTS & Free level 4 -HC - Free level 3 / HC level 3

5. The POS Schedule (after-life i.e., after 80+) - All HC completed.

The SS (40+–80+) takes 40+ years to reach the POS schedule (after life, i.e., after 80+). We may write the after-life date, month, year and time.

My POS Schedule (after-life) is the highest knowledge for MYSELF. My POS schedule (after-life) is about being FREE from all. After following my POS in my SS (40+ to 80+), my all HC Results are received/completed by my POS.

Following my POS is completed in my POS Schedule (after-life). My POS in my POS Schedule (after-life) completes all my SS. The POS Schedule is to know/ understand my SS and my POS; my POS is the last in the hierarchy. After following my POS, my POS gives myself the understanding of my POS Schedule (after-life).

As there is MIND, there is YOU/SELF/FREE too. YOU know FREE after following the HC thoughts chanting and the HSOM (for around 30 years). Similarly, as there is YOU/Self/Free, there is FREE from all. Self/YOU know free from all by surrender.

Knowing that higher than YOU/Self/Free in the hierarchy is FREE from all, i.e., my billions, my Supreme and my POS are higher in the hierarchy than YOU/SELF are. Free from all means free from YOU/Self and thus to go to my POS, my POS is the last in the hierarchy. Free from all means to know/understand my POS.

It takes around 30 years to know FREE after following the HC thoughts chanting and the HSOM Exercise in the PS and the RS. YOU/Self again want to attach with the HC Results at around 40 years, in the SS (40+ to 80+). Results are not your part, it's the POS's part; this knowledge is free from all HC results.

Would YOU/SELF/FREE take another 40 years (my SS 40+ to 80+) to know/accept free from all/my supreme/ my POS? YOU/SELF should know that after surrendering all my HC Results and myself, my POS is harmoniously working for my all HC Results and myself, NOW, until the last. As it is free, there is free from all. Similarly, there is FREE from all. Surrender is the only refuge free from my all HC Results and free from MYSELF.

Why free from all?

By birth, Self/YOU was one with all the billions, one with my SUPREME, filled with complete surrender because FREE from all is an eternal search of YOU/Self/ Free. After following my POS, my POS gives YOU/SELF the understanding of my POS Schedule. The understanding of my POS schedule given by my POS is Free from all. By following my POS, Self/YOU again becomes one with all the billions, one with my SUPREME.

After following my POS, my POS gives understanding to YOU/Self which knows that if SELF/YOU/Free is so harmonious, then how harmonious is free from all, i.e., identify how harmonious is my BILLIONS and my SUPREME (Supreme is free from all). We billions are one with SUPREME, ONE in ALL and ALL in ONE.

My SUPREME is free from all HC Results, and my SUPREME gives all my HC Results through my billions. After following my POS (40+ to 80+), my POS makes myself harmonious to know/understand my POS schedule (free from all). Moreover, it makes myself harmonious to know/understand my POS, of how harmonious my POS is, which gives the understanding of the POS schedule (after-life).

Wonder how HARMONIOUS is my POS because ONLY my POS makes all the things, all my 7.4+ billions and my SUPREME harmonious, thus all my HC Results come to me by themselves and my POS is now completed/ receives all my HC Results. This is the way of working of my POS, i.e., to make everything harmonious.

FREE turns into gratitude to my billions and my Supreme.

Free from all (free from my HC Results and free from myself) turns into surrender to my POS. Knowing/ understanding of Free from all turns into a complete surrendering bow to my POS by MYSELF.

I have known/understood what is its eternal search, i.e., free from all. Knowing/understanding of the Free from all turns into a complete surrendering bow to my POS by MYSELF.

My POS Schedule is the highest knowledge and the knowledge about the hierarchy, which comes after YOU/ Self, i.e., we billions, my Supreme. My POS schedule is the complete surrender to my POS by MYSELF in REAL.

My POS Schedule afterlife (free from all) is the manifested, infinite, deepest and purest form of my POS. My POS schedule after-life is free from all. Self/YOU have known my POS schedule (after-life), i.e., My POS schedule afterlife is free from all. Self/YOU have known that my POS is harmoniously working with my all HC Results.

Come back to my Supreme Schedule –

My SS is a live form of free from all in REAL, i.e., it's my POS.

It's a KNOWING. It's a KNOWING of my POS given by my POS only.

Wonder how harmonious is my POS. Wonder how harmoniously my POS is working. Wonder how harmoniously my POS is working with YOU. Wonder how harmoniously my POS is working for my HC Result NOW........$ for my purpose.

A complete surrendering bow to you my POS, by MYSELF.

It's all by following my POS.

Be with my POS. My POS is MIRACULOUS.

A complete surrendering bow to you my POS, by MYSELF and from all the 7.4+ billion.

There may be left some bondage (questions/worry/doubt/fear).

Let's go again to my POS schedule (afterlife, i.e., after 80+).

Self/ YOU have known the harmonious workings of my POS for my all HC Results by my POS and for a refuge for myself.

Self/YOU should know now that after following my POS for around 40 years (my SS is 40+–80+) two times daily, morning/evening daily, after waking up& before sleeping, 1/2 hour each, and after 40 years of being with my POS. All day, all my SS (including all my HC Results NOW and all my HC Results NOW related things) is completed/received by my POS in my POS schedule (after-life);a complete surrendering bow, my POS.

Come back to my Supreme Schedule again.

Self/YOU give a live form of a complete surrendering bow to my POS by myself and by all the 7.4+ billions. Self falls in LOVE with my POS. A complete surrendering bow to my POS, for my POS is giving me refuge, and completing/receiving my all HC Results NOW.

From my POS schedule (after-life), Self/YOU know that my POS is harmoniously working NOW for my all HC Results NOW and all my HC Results NOW are already completed/received by my POS in my POS schedule (after-life).

YOU/Self have to do nothing for real now; YOU/Self is only a witness now (after following my POS).

After HC thoughts chanting, HC ideas, knowing and understanding, hence finally coming to following my POS.

HOW is clear now. This is the HC level 3/FREE level 3.

MY POS–FREE level 4

Bhagavad Gita

Sarva-guhyatamam bhuyah srnu me paramam vacah isto 'si me drdham iti tato vaksyami te hitam man-mana bhava mad-bhakto mad-yaji mam namaskuru mam evaisyasi satyam te pratijane priyo 'si me sarva-

dharman parityajya mam ekam saranam vrajaaham tvam sarva-papebhyo moksayisyami ma sucah

Hear again, my supreme word, the most mysterious of all; dearly beloved thou art of Me,

Hence I desire to declare thy welfare. On Me, fix thy mind; to Me, bring thy devotion;to Me, offer thy sacrifice; to Me, make thy obeisance; to Me indeed shalt thou come—solemn is My promise to thee, thou art dear to Me.

Abandon all duties and come to Me, the only refuge.

My POS told me now, what, why, when & HOW; all is clear.

My POS told me, now don't mention my HC Results Now during following my POS.

My POS told me, mention my HC Results Now after following my POS.

My POS told me, follow my POS, for my POS only.

I asked my POS, what else should I do for you, my POS.

I asked my POS, may I chant you till the last, my POS.

My POS told me, no need to chant now.

My POS told me, keep following my POS, for my POS only.

(i.e., From my PS, my RS and now in my SS, it's my POS.

My POS told me, Faith and Gratitude is born from Surrender.)

My POS asked me, if I didn't get my HC Result NOW and all my HC Results NO, will I follow my POS then?

I said, YES, my POS.

My POS asked me, why?

I will follow you, my POS, because I love you, my POS.

I'll follow you, my POS, for you only, my POS.

I'll follow you, my POS, till my last, for you only, my POS.

I'll follow you, my POS, because I want to be with you, my POS.

I'll come again & again for you, my POS.

I'll follow you, my POS, because by following you, I have all this good understanding, and you gave me this good understanding to follow you, my POS.

It's my POS, it's all by following you, my POS.

I will now declare to thee, who art uncensorious, this mysterious knowledge, together with discriminative knowledge, knowing which thou shalt be released from all. This is the king of sciences, the king of mysteries, pure and sovereign, capable of direct comprehension, the essence of dharma, easy to practice, changeless.

- Bhagavad Gita

My POS told me, after following my POS, for my POS only, it's my POS.

My POS told me, my POS is the secret of secrets, the most mysterious of all, the last & final in the hierarchy, the FREE level 4.

I asked my POS, how do I know it's you, my POS?

My POS told me, when it's my POS, then all the bondage (questions, worry, doubt fear) is cleared by my POS and then in real, there remain no question.

My POS told me and I am talking with you.

My POS told me, mostly all the questions are answered.

My POS told me, if I want to know/clear something, then I should go back to read (my PS, RS) my SS and then come back here.

Follow my POS for my POS only, m/e daily, a/w &b/s,2 times, mor/eve, 10-15 minutes each, till the last, 40+ years.

Close your eyes and sit in a comfortable posture.

Start with talking with my POS -

My POS told me, follow my POS for my POS only.

My POS told me, after following my POS for my POS only, it's my POS- the free level 4 .

My POS told me, my POS is the secret of secrets, the most mysterious of all, the last & final in the hierarchy, the free level 4.

I LOVE you, my POS.

My POS told me, the FREE level 4 is Loving my POS.

I LOVE you, my POS.I LOVE you, my POS.

Then, my POS chanting, it's my POS, it's all by (following) my POS (5-8 minutes in a singing way and head moving left and right).

Then, after my POS chanting, surrendering to my POS -

A complete surrendering bow to you, my POS; we billions love you, my POS. Our families give a complete surrendering bow to you, my BILLIONS; our families love you, my BILLIONS.

WE BILLIONS give a complete surrendering bow to you, my SUPREME; WE BILLIONS love you, my SUPREME; WE BILLIONS give a complete surrendering bow to you, my POS;WE BILLIONS love you, my POS.

Then, after surrendering to my POS, my POS gives me surrenderness.

Surrenderness is loving my POS. Surrenderness is a complete surrendering bow to my POS.

During surrenderness, there is no chanting. Pause my POS chanting for 5-8 minutes.

Then, after surrenderness, my POS told me, after surrenderness, it's my POS–the FREE level 4.

My POS told me, my POS is the secret of secrets, the most mysterious of all, the last & final in the hierarchy, the free level 4.

I LOVE you, my POS. **My POS told me, the FREE level 4 is Loving my POS.**

I LOVE you, my POS. I LOVE you, my POS.

My POS told me, following my POS is now complete for my POS only. Open your eyes now.

My POS told me, as YOU follow the POS for my POS only, the MIND also fell in LOVE with the POS.

MY POS told me, write down my SS & HC RESULT NOW in my SS.

MY POS, my SS and my HC RESULT NOW in my SS -

My Supreme Schedule (SS) – (40+–80+ = 40 years)

A.HOW–by my POS.

1.Follow my POS for my POS only, m/e daily, a/w&b/s, around 4 AM, around 10 PM, 10-15 minutes, till the last.

1.My POS told me, rest all the time after following my POS for my POS only, it's my POS- the FREE level 4.

I LOVE you, my POS. My POS told me, the Free level 4 is Loving my POS.

(I'll chant only, "I LOVE you, my POS," and only as my LOVE for my POS daily, time to time, till my last.

1.Brahamcharya and LOVE–LOVE is always an Inspiration.

BS–Set your Brahamcharya Schedule, have good friends.

4.Constant min. action/effort everyday for my HC Result NOW.

5.Visualization of my SS- sometimes only .

B.WHEN& C. WHAT–NOW

My HC Result NOW–........................

My next HC Result NOW–................

My next HC Result NOW -....................

D–PURPOSE (WHY) -............................

My POS told me, all my SS(including my HC Result NOW) is coming to me itself, NOW, in reality and abundance by LOVING my POS.

{My POS told me coming = setting my SS, receiving, maintaining, sustaining, completing and the completed, thus all the completed in my SS (my SS includes my all HC Results NOW and HC Results NOW related things)till the last for forty years by LOVING my POS.}

My POS, I want my .... $, NOW, for my purpose.

My POS told me, my .... $ and all my SS is coming to me itself, NOW, in reality & abundance by LOVING my POS.

My POS then told me my next HC Result NOW and all my SS, by LOVING my POS.

My POS schedule (after life, i.e., after 80) -

My POS told me, all my SS is complete/received in my POS schedule (after life) by LOVING my POS*.

LOVING my POS*-

My POS told me, loving my POS is -

Following my POS for my POS only.

1. Chanting only, 'I LOVE you, my POS,' and only as my LOVE for my POS, time to time daily. My POS told me the gap time between chanting is also loving my POS.

2. My POS told me, doing my purpose is also loving my POS.

3. Loving the way my POS took over my mind and my self, and thus my POS is harmoniously working/giving my HC Result NOW/my SS.

My POS is the deepest NOW. NOW is born from timelessness/ the deepest Now. YOU/FREE/NOW wants to keep attached with my HC Result NOW/all SS. Self/YOU/ NOW wants to use all its energy, knowledge, understanding to receive itself your HC Result NOW.

My POS told me, YOU/free/NOW/my HC Result NOW/ all my SS is ONE. My POS is NOW as well as the deepest NOW.

YOU/Self/Free have nothing to do with the HC Results NOW because RESULTS part is not your part.

My POS told me, YOU do your minimum effort everyday.

The RESULTS part is my POS's part. This is the deepest NOW/timeless NOW. This is loving my POS.

4. After surrendering to my POS, it's my POS, the deepest now, the free level 4.YOU/NOW become passive for your HC Results NOW/all my SS, while my POS becomes active for my HC Results NOW part/for my all SS. This is loving my POS.

My POS told me, believing (at a mental level) in my POS is loving my POS.

My POS told me, the deepest NOW/FREE level 4 is loving my POS.

Love my POS because my POS is the last & final in the hierarchy. Love my POS to be ONE with my POS.

LOVE my POS because my POS wants only my LOVE to give me all my SS in reality and abundance, NOW.

My POS told me, LOVE my POS because my POS wants only my LOVE, and LOVING my POS means my POS comp/received all my SS in my POS schedule (after life)

My POS told me, as my POS comp/received all my SS in my POS schedule (after life),NOW, I'm chanting only 'I LOVE YOU, my POS,' only as my LOVE for my POS till the last, i.e., my SS (40+–80+ years).

My POS told me, SELF knows it's my POS only after following my POS, for my POS and MIND know chanting only I LOVE YOU, my POS, which is the free level 4.

Thus, my POS told me, following my POS for my POS only is loving my POS by my SELF & chanting only I LOVE YOU, my POS, only as my LOVE for my POS, is LOVING my POS by my MIND.

5. My POS told me, because the RESULTS part (all my SS) is not my Part, it's my POS' part. So, LOVING my POS is only my LOVE for my POS (following &chanting). My POS is harmoniously working for all my SS. My POS set/following my SS gave me earlier the HC Result Now, and is giving me my HC Result NOW——$, and will give me next my HC Result NOW.

6. My POS told me, now I & SELF have become ONE with my POS.

My POS told me, LOVING my POS is by my POS.

My POS told me, LOVING my POS means it's my POS.

My POS told me, it's my POS means I have already got all my SS.

My POS told as I already got all my SS, it's only left, loving my POS, i.e, following my POS for my POS only, for SELF and chanting only–I Love You, my POS, for my Love for my POS, for MIND.

My POS told me, the GAP time between chanting is also LOVING my POS.

My POS told me, LOVING my POS because my POS wants my LOVE only through following my POS and through my POS chanting.

About the Author

The author has studied and researched the religious and inspirational book GITA for 20 years, started following its principles at a young age, and has continued to follow the harmonious schedules explained in this book till NOW.

The book is a complete guide for the young aged (14 - 30), middle aged (30 - 40) and for 40+ to 80+ aged.

This book is the result of what the author understands from the book GITA and the writings of the greats, from past and present.

Printed by Libri Plureos GmbH in Hamburg,
Germany